LYNN RAYE

NEW YORK TIMES & USA TODAY BESTSELLING AUTHOR

HARRIS

RECKLESS
HEAT

*Prequel to HOT PURSUIT,
a Hostile Operations Team Novel*

Copyright ©2016 by Lynn Raye Harris
Cover Design © 2016 Croco Designs

www.**lynnrayeharris**.com

First Edition: February 2016
Library of Congress Cataloging-in-Publication Data

Harris, Lynn Raye
    Reckless Heat / Lynn Raye Harris. – 1st ed
        ISBN-13: 978-1-941002-13-1

                    1.   Reckless Heat—Fiction
                        2.   Fiction—Romance
                3.   Fiction—Contemporary Romance

OTHER BOOKS IN
THE *HOSTILE OPERATIONS TEAM* SERIES

RECKLESS HEAT

Prequel to HOT PURSUIT,
a Hostile Operations Team Novel

CHAPTER
ONE

Evie

Ten years before the events of Hot Pursuit...

I'VE BEEN IN love with Matt Girard since I was eleven and he cried on my shoulder after his mama's funeral. That's the first moment I realized that what I felt for him has the ability to rock my world to its foundation. I knew then that we were meant to be together.

Matt doesn't know what's going to happen yet, but I've always believed he'll realize the truth in time. Except I just heard a rumor he's leaving town after graduation. For good.

My stomach is tight, my heart is pounding, and I feel light-headed as I walk down the halls of Rochambeau High, searching for him.

I met Matt when I was six and he was seven. My mama is a hairdresser and she'd been driving out to Reynier's Retreat, Matt's family home, to fix his mother's hair once a week. Margaret Anne Girard was very sick, though I didn't understand it at the time. She wanted her hair done, and Mama made the trip out there to style it for her.

One day Mama took me with her. The Girards are wealthy, so Matt and his sister Christina didn't go to public school like I did. I'd never talked to them before.

Seeing that big house up close awed me. It was the grandest house I'd ever seen, and I was certain the people in it would be different from me. Better, I guess. Perfectly groomed and gleaming like they were made of gold.

But then Matt appeared on the veranda. His hair was sticking up, he was dirty and disheveled, and he held a worm in his hand. He marched over to me and tried to scare me by waving it in my face. When I didn't scream or run, he dropped it down my shirt. He thought I was going to lose my shit then, but of course I didn't. I just fished the worm out and said it was a waste of good bait.

He grinned at me—and that's the moment we became best friends. Since then, we've gotten dirty together, gone skinny-dipping, dared each other to do things that would horrify our parents (like the summer he turned fourteen and stole his daddy's car for a joyride to Baton Rouge. Thank God we didn't get caught!), and generally been inseparable for much of our childhood.

But then I got breasts and hips, and Matt didn't even notice. I thought maybe he was pretending not to at first, but I never once caught him looking at me like I was a girl rather than one of the guys.

When he finally started going to public school, I thought that would be the perfect chance for us to see each other more often. He couldn't help but realize I was a girl then, right?

Wrong-o. We hung out less and less as he made other friends—and started seeing other girls. I was stunned. What do they have that I don't? I have boobs. I have hips. I even wear makeup! My hair is long and thick and shiny, not boyish at all.

But no, he's never noticed me that way. Instead, Matt has girlfriends—lots of girlfriends. I watch them together with a combination of hurt and jealousy and bewilderment—seriously, what is the deal? Why are they different?

I haven't a clue, and I've cried into my pillow more nights than I remember.

But one thing gives me hope. Matt always moves on. He never stays with any of them. I think, deep down, he must know that none of those girls are the one for him. They can't be, because I'm the one. He just hasn't figured it out yet.

Now I don't know if he ever will.

I find him near his locker. Jeanine Jackson is there, giggling and flirting with him. She has her hands behind her and she's leaning back against the lockers, arching her back so her breasts thrust forward.

She's cute in a perky blonde way, and Matt is clearly interested. They dated last summer for a short time. He brought her out to Charlie's Diner one night when I was waiting tables, and she had the nerve to tell me not to talk to her boyfriend unless I was taking his order.

Like she was anything more than the flavor of the week. Matt told her to chill out, but that didn't stop her from glaring daggers at me. I might have *accidentally* dumped a pitcher of sweet tea on her a few minutes later. That chilled her the fuck out for sure.

Bitch.

And now Matt's ogling her breasts and looking like he might take her out again. Fucking hell, I can't get a break where this boy is concerned. My life feels like it's falling apart, and he doesn't have the first clue.

"Hey, Matt," I say, and he looks up, meeting my gaze. He doesn't smile, and that tightens the ball in my stomach even more. My throat is dry and my head feels like it might explode.

"Hey, Evie," he says, but he takes a step back from Jeanine. She's glaring at me, of course.

"Could I, uh, talk to you for a second? Alone," I add when Jeanine's mouth tightens.

It's bold of me, and I have no idea if he'll agree, but really, what do I have to lose? If he's truly leaving town, then everything's going sideways and I don't give a fuck about anything else.

"Sure." He reaches into his locker and grabs his backpack, then shuts it and turns to Jeanine. "See you later, *cher*."

Jeanine clutches his arm. "I was hoping you could give me a ride home," she purrs.

"Can't today, babe. Not going your way."

He turns away, dismissing her that easily, and heads for my side. If looks could kill, I'd be dead, because Jeanine clearly hates me right this second.

I resist the urge to stick my tongue out, but barely. I settle for an arched eyebrow and a slight smirk instead. Jeanine gets it because her eyes promise retribution.

"Whatcha want, Evie-girl?" Matt asks as he starts down the hallway.

I walk alongside him, my throat still tight, and wonder how to get the words out. We're almost to the doors when I finally manage it. "I, uh, heard you were leaving town."

He stops and turns to me. My heart skips a beat. He's so handsome, so tall and beautiful. I love his face, the strong lines of his jaw and nose. His eyes are silvery gray. His black hair is cut tight lately, but I know it curls when it's longer. I want to touch it, but I don't dare.

"That's right," he says, and my heart practically stops before it starts galloping again. I'm his oldest friend, dammit, and he didn't even tell me. "I got an appointment to the United States Military Academy at West Point."

"West Point." I say it dully because I'm stunned. I thought he was going to LSU. He used to talk about being a Tiger when we were younger, about playing football and studying something that would enable him to help people.

But West Point? The military?

His eyes are bleak, and it breaks my heart. I want to hug him. I don't feel like I have that right, so I don't.

"Wow," I finally force out. "Not what I expected."

"Not what a lot of people expected, I imagine."

I'm pretty sure he's talking about his father now. Matt and his dad have never gotten along well. I know his dad drinks a bit, and I was there once when he yelled at Matt and told him to get the fuck out of the house. I also know Matt wasn't happy that his dad remarried less than a year after his mother died. Matt didn't like his first stepmother—and who could blame him?

Senator Girard—he's a Louisiana state senator, not a United States senator—married a woman that Mama said came straight from the strip club. Then he divorced that one and married another one. He divorced the second one about a year ago now.

I don't think Senator Girard's second and third wives were very motherly toward his children. What makes me think that? Well, Christina is a sad girl who doesn't talk a lot, and Matt has grown a bit reckless over the years.

He might party a bit much, and of course he drinks beer and stuff—but who doesn't? So far as I know, he only stole his daddy's car that one time, so I don't think he takes crazy risks. He definitely goes out with the wrong girls, which I hate, but he never stays with them long.

He's not a delinquent by any stretch. He's just rich and maybe a bit spoiled in ways, but I trust that he knows how far he can go before he crosses the line.

"Maaatttt," a voice calls, and I turn to see Tiffany Blessing coming our way.

Matt swears under his breath and heads for the doors without acknowledging her. He throws a look over his shoulder right before he bangs through the doors. I'm still standing in place like a deer in headlights. Still processing what he said about West Point.

"You coming or what?"

Of course I'm going with him. My feet start to move, carrying me out the doors and into the parking lot. Matt unlocks his shiny red Corvette and jumps inside. I do the same. I don't know where we're going, and I don't care. We're together, just us. Just like old times.

He revs the engine and peels out of the lot like there's a monster on our tail. Students stop to watch us go by. The girls look longingly at us. The boys don't see anything but the car.

Elation swells inside me, but I know it won't last. Matt whips the car onto the highway and heads in the opposite direction from town. He turns up the radio as it

6

blasts Green Day. It's too loud to speak, so I don't even try.

I glance at Matt, at the way he grips the wheel, his fingers long and sure. His jaw is set in a stubborn line, and his eyebrows are two sharp slashes on his forehead. He's irritated, but I don't know why.

Eventually he turns onto a dirt road I recognize. It's not far from Reynier's Retreat, and it heads down a forest road, emerging on a small bluff over the bayou. It's a breathtaking sight and one I haven't seen in a few years now.

The afternoon sunshine is slanting through the trees, highlighting the bugs that swirl in the light. When we reach the small clearing, Matt pulls the car up a couple of feet near the edge, powers the windows down, and cuts the engine.

He puts his wrists on top of the wheel and sits there, staring out. He makes no move to open the door. So I don't either. I watch the bugs and the shadowy form of a gator sliding through the murky swamp beneath the cypresses.

"I love this place," Matt says, startling me. "It's peaceful."

"It is." It's also filled with memories. We used to sneak off down here in his little motorboat, long before I was in the accident this past summer that made me scared of boats and water, and we used to lie on this bank in the sun, eating the snacks we'd brought and making up tricks to play on Christina.

Life was simple back then. It wasn't simple anymore.

"We had some good times here, didn't we?"

"We did."

He sighs and turns his head to look at me. His arms are still draped over the wheel, and his biceps flex as he clenches a fist over and over. "I won't ever forget you, Evie."

My heart thumps. It sounds like good-bye. I don't like it. "I hope not."

"I'll stay in touch when I can. And I'll be back on breaks."

I latch onto that single thought and let the joy inside me peek out of the box it's trapped in. I need something positive to hold on to while my heart's breaking. "You will?"

"Why wouldn't I?"

"I don't know… I heard you were leaving for good."

I'd be happier if he looked surprised, but he doesn't. He looks… guilty? Confused? I don't know, but it squashes the joy and replaces it with anxiety.

"I'm not leaving for good," he says, looking at the bayou again. "But I doubt I'll ever move back to Rochambeau. There's nothing I want here."

Of course that hurts. Why wouldn't it? I love him, and it's clear he doesn't feel the same.

And why would he? We've never even kissed. He doesn't look at me that way, though I keep hoping. But I'm just not as pretty as the other girls. I don't have buck-teeth anymore, but I'm not petite and cute like Jeanine or even my cousin Julie. I'm tall and awkward. I tower over many of the girls in my class.

And Matt's not interested. He doesn't see me that way and never has. I'm beginning to fear he never will.

I sniff and turn my head to look at the water glinting in the sunlight. What can I say? I can't tell him how much

8

those words hurt me. I damn sure can't tell him how I feel about him. He won't laugh at me. Definitely not.

He'll pity me, and that would be infinitely worse.

"I miss this," I say instead. "Coming out here with you. Talking about stuff. It's been a long time."

He heaves a sigh. "It has been. I'm sorry about that."

"You've been busy."

"Yeah."

He reaches over then and takes my hand, and I think I might come unglued. Every touch from Matt Girard is one to be savored, treasured, taken out and reexamined when I'm lonely or sad.

And this is the first one in a long, long time.

"You've been a good friend, Evie. The best. You'll always be a part of my life no matter where I go."

I squeeze his hand as emotion flows through me. I'm not ready to let him go yet, but what choice do I have?

Unless I think up something quick, something that will change his mind or make him see me as more than a friend, I have none.

Absolutely none.

"That's good," I say, my throat tight.

CHAPTER TWO

Matt

I'M HOLDING EVIE'S hand, and I need to let go before I do something I'll regret. I disentangle myself from her and stare out the window at the bayou.

My life is so fucked up I sometimes can't believe it. How did it get this way? How did I get to this place where I mostly feel numb inside?

I shouldn't be numb. I should be on top of the fucking world.

It looks like I have a perfect life. My father is Beau Girard, state senator, oilman. He's got buckets of money. Mountains of money. We live in a house that was built in the 1850s by one of our ancestors. It's a grand old plantation home with huge columns along the front and antiques in every room. It's about sixteen thousand square feet—and it feels empty to me, in spite of the rooms packed with rich furnishings.

It hasn't felt like a home since my mother died. That

was five years ago. The old man married again—twice—but neither of them worked out.

That's the polite way of putting it. I feel a pang whenever I think of Candy, stepmama number two. Jesus, but she did a mind fuck on me. What sixteen-year-old wouldn't fuck a hot twenty-two-year-old stripper if given the chance? She wasn't my first, but she damn sure was the best.

Candy played on my senses, on my naiveté. Of course I was naive. I hate admitting that, but it's true. I thought we were some sort of star-crossed lovers.

I was dumb enough to think I loved her. And she was spiteful enough to let me believe she loved me in return. It was all a game to her. When the old man gave her a large divorce settlement, she laughed in my face when I asked her about us. Told me to grow up and get over it.

Jesus, I hate that woman. And, yeah, I'm embarrassed on some level that I was so stupid. It happened over a year ago now, but I don't think the old man knows. He never said anything about it, and I've stopped caring if he does. Our problems are far bigger than Candy.

Evie doesn't say anything, but I can feel her looking at me. Sweet little Evie. I don't dare look at her right now. I know she's upset with me and trying her best not to cry. Hell, I know she has a crush on me. I've never wanted that, not from her, but it happened anyway.

I'm not going to encourage it. I'm not an asshole—well, not a total asshole—and I'm not taking advantage of her feelings. Not Evie.

"Are you dating Jeanine again?" she asks, and a current of relief rolls through me that she's moved on from the serious side of this conversation.

I feel safe enough to look at her again. A jolt hits me right between the eyes when I do. It's almost as if I've never looked at her before when in fact I've looked at her a thousand—a million—times. I've watched her grow up, for fuck's sake. There's nothing new here.

And yet she's got the prettiest eyes I've ever seen. They're so blue they're almost purple, and she's wearing a purple T-shirt that clings to her curves and dips down not quite far enough for me to see cleavage but enough to jump-start my imagination.

Her black hair is straight, thick, and shiny. She's shoved it behind her ears, and I have an urge to fan my hands into it and spread it over her shoulders just to see how long and full it really is.

She's looking at me quizzically, and I realize I've been silent for too long.

"Not really," I say. And it's true. I'm not dating Jeanine—I'm not dating anyone—but I won't turn down pussy when it's offered. I have sense enough to know it'll probably be a lot more difficult to get some action at West Point since my time will be so tightly controlled to start with.

"She doesn't like me."

I can't help but snort a laugh. "You dumped tea on her. Of course she doesn't like you."

"She's probably planning her revenge right now for my stealing you away this afternoon."

I didn't think of that but, yeah, probably right. Jeanine has always been vindictive. "I'll fix it," I tell her.

She's looking at me with a frown creasing her pretty face. "How are you going to…?"

I don't want to tell her that it'll involve Jeanine naked

and spread beneath me, so I don't.

"I just will. I'll make her forget all about it, promise."

She stares at me another moment, and then she starts to turn red. Evie's not dumb, that's for sure.

"Don't do me any favors, Matt. In fact, save it, because your dick might fall off if you stick it in that skank's coochie."

Oh my God, I want to fucking laugh my ass off. I don't because I sense it'll only piss her off. Not to mention that I'm oddly turned on by hearing Evie say the word dick. I want her to say it again.

No you don't, asshole.

On second thought, maybe I don't.

"I'll wear a condom," I say and then wonder why in the hell I'm going down this road. Talking sex with Evie is not a good idea.

Evie lowers her gaze and bites her lip. Fucking hell.

"You're embarrassed," I say. "I'm sorry."

She lifts her head then, her eyes flashing. "I'm not embarrassed—I just think you could do much better than Jeanine."

"I'm not marrying her, Evie."

She folds her arms over her middle, lifting her breasts up. I don't think she knows that's the effect, but I sure am enjoying it. More than I should.

"I certainly hope not."

A thought occurs to me as I take in her discomfort. Because no matter what she says, she *is* uncomfortable. I've never really thought about it before, except in passing here and there, but now the truth hits me over the head like a hammer.

"Are you still a virgin, Evie?"

Her eyes widen and her cheeks redden, and I know I've hit the jackpot. I don't know why, but it makes me happy. It shouldn't matter one way or the other, but it does.

"Are you going to make fun of me if I say yes?"

"I wouldn't do that, Evie-girl. I think you know that."

She drops her gaze again. "It's not that I haven't had the opportunity—but no, I've never…"

Her voice trails off, and I know what she can't say. "Had sex," I finish for her.

She nods.

I can't help what I do next. I put a finger beneath her chin and tip her head up until she's looking at me. My God, I feel so many confusing things when my eyes meet this girl's. She's like a little sister to me—and she's not like a sister at all. She's someone I want to protect, and someone I want to taste and touch and hold.

I'll only do one of those things though.

"There's nothing to be ashamed of, Evie. Don't let anyone rush you into it, okay? Do it when it feels right to you."

CHAPTER THREE

Evie

I WANT TO tell him it feels right, right *now*, but I can't form the words. And he won't take me up on it anyway. My heart hammers and my skin tingles where he touches, but this is as much stimulation as I'm going to get from Matt Girard.

I wish I was brave enough to close the distance between us and press my lips to his, but I'm not. Instead, I hold my breath and stare into his eyes and pray—*pray*—he'll make the first move.

He smiles at me, a soft curling of his lips, and my pulse quickens. He's everything I ever wanted in a guy, but he doesn't look at me that way at all. I can see it in his smile, feel it in the way his finger rests beneath my chin. There's no reciprocation here.

He sometimes looks at me with a hard, faraway look, but it doesn't last long. Faraway and friendly are his two settings for me. It is what it is, no matter that I wish it was more.

He leans away, dropping his finger, and my heart aches with disappointment.

"You ready to get home?" he asks, but he's starting the car without waiting for my reply.

I nod, because an answer isn't really needed. He turns around and heads back out to the road. Again, he cranks up the music, Creed this time, and we fly toward town.

We go down Main Street, past the shop where Mama works—she's going to buy it someday—past the old general store and the café, and then he turns and heads for the railroad tracks that divide Rochambeau in two. First we pass through the historic district, filled with old homes, huge trees, and pristine lawns, before driving over the tracks and into the poorer section of town.

My section. I shouldn't be embarrassed. After all, Matt's been here before. He's seen the little home I live in, the dirt driveway, the ramshackle siding, the clothesline that hangs near the house, and he's never said a negative word about any of it.

We pull up to the house, his shiny Corvette seeming out of place, and Julie walks outside. She's got Sarah, my six-year-old sister, with her. Sarah waves like mad and Matt waves back. Sarah knows Matt, but not too well since he never comes over anymore. But she hasn't forgotten.

"Thanks for the ride home," I say, wrapping my hand around the door handle.

He swings his silvery gaze to me. He looks sad, but I don't know why. "I won't forget you, Evie-girl. We'll always be friends."

My throat is too tight to speak, so I just nod. I step out of the car and he backs out of the driveway. I stand there until the Corvette is gone.

CHAPTER
FOUR

Matt

I JACK THE car up to a hundred miles per hour. It's dangerous for more than one reason. First, it's a two-lane road with sharp bends and trees that obscure the view up ahead and make for short sight distances. Second, you can never tell when something might run out in front of you. It isn't dark yet, which means the chances are less than if it had been, but it's still a risk.

And then there's the possibility of coming up too fast on a slower car around a bend. Someone could get hurt.

Reluctantly, I slow my speed. Three more weeks and I'm out of here. Three more weeks of enduring my life before it changes forever.

I can't fucking wait. And I don't need to screw it up before it happens. It wasn't easy getting into West Point.

I did the entire application process with the school counselor. I left the old man out of it, though it would have been easier to get the recommendation of the state's representative to Congress if I'd asked my father for help.

I didn't want his help. I told Mr. Biggs that I wanted to do it on my own, wanted to surprise my old man with my initiative and ingenuity. If I didn't get in, no big deal, I said—it wasn't like I wouldn't go to college if I didn't. But if I did, then it was something I did without my father's help.

And something I could do without his interference. Truthfully, it *was* a big deal to me—and now I'm in and I'm not fucking it up.

I turn down the lane leading to Reynier's Retreat. The trees lining the drive are old, dripping with moss, and obscure the view of the house. When it appears at the end of the lane, it's impressive. A monument to history and privilege.

I love it and hate it in equal measure. I stop the car and look at the house. General John Hamilton Girard grew up in this house before going off to fight in the Civil War. He'd been my age, seventeen, when he joined. He had a triumphant career and then returned a hero.

A figure comes out to stand on the massive veranda. It's my father, staring down the drive as if he's been waiting for me. I step on the gas and drive the rest of the way to the house. I put the car in the garage and go inside.

My father's in the kitchen as I walk in, tumbler of whiskey in one hand, eyes bloodshot. I'm used to the disappointment on his face, but it doesn't mean I'm unaffected.

"West Point." He's slurring. "You're too soft for fucking West Point, boy."

"Yes, sir." This is my stock answer because it's no use arguing with him. He hasn't let up on this refrain since

I got the news a couple of weeks ago.

"Are you sassing me?"

"No, sir." I stand with my backpack slung over one shoulder, clenching a fist at my side. I'm taller than he is, but the senator is bigger. More muscular.

He takes a slug of the whiskey. "Damned disappointment from the day you were born, you know that? Sissy boy always running to his fucking mother. Crying when anyone said boo. Fucking pussy."

The blood rises up hot and hard in my veins. My cheeks flush. I can feel it, feel the sweat and the anger as it singes my pores. Goddamn but I want to throat-punch the bastard.

Or tell him I fucked his wife. Candy didn't think I was a pussy when she was screaming my name and begging me to fuck her harder.

Telling him that wouldn't do a damned bit of good though. He'd probably find a way to stop me from leaving after graduation, and there's no way in hell I'm letting that happen.

I just have to keep my cool for three more weeks. The old man is home and drunk today, but he'll just as likely be gone tomorrow. Off to a strip club or to Girard Oil. He runs the company when he's sober, leaves it to his board when he's on a bender.

This is a bender week apparently.

"I'm sorry, sir." I'll say whatever it takes to shut him the fuck up. To get him to leave me alone and lose himself in that glass.

He leans against the kitchen island, and I know he's really been drinking today. He needs the island for support.

"Sorry," he slurs. "Always sorry. For fucking what? Being born a pussy?"

I stiffen, but no way in hell am I letting him get to me. "Yes, sir. I'm sorry I'm a pussy."

That's too much, and I know it the second I say it. But it's too late now. The old man draws himself up, his red eyes gleaming hot. He slams the glass on the counter and closes the distance between us.

I know what's coming. It isn't the first time. It doesn't happen often, but it happens enough.

He rears back and slaps me across the face. He's never punched me. Never. But the old man is king of the gentlemanly slap. As if he's challenging me to a duel.

It fucking hurts, of course. Snaps my head to the side and stings my cheek. I feel a hot bite of something more, and I lift my hand to my face. It comes away red.

His college ring caught me on my cheekbone and sliced the skin.

My father is standing there with that wild-ass look on his face, glaring at me. Time seems suspended. And then he does what he always does when he's slapped me.

He collapses against me, hugging me hard, crying the very tears he accused me of being a pussy for. "I'm sorry, son. I didn't mean it... I didn't mean it."

He'll go on like this for a while if I let him. I wrap my arms around him and swallow the massive knot in my throat. I hate him. And I don't. It's a fucking sorry place to be most of the time.

"You need to lie down, sir," I say. "Sleep it off."

I'm not afraid he'll explode now. Once he has his meltdown, he's done until the next time. He continues sobbing on my shoulder while I maneuver him over to the couch in the family room. I settle him on it, take off his shoes and lift his feet to the sofa, then straighten and look down at him.

His eyes are red rimmed, the lids swollen. He gazes up at me bleary-eyed. "Look like your mother," he whispers, and my heart pinches tight. "I miss her so much sometimes. Hurts looking at you."

"Yes, sir." I have no sympathy for him, not really. It's always about him, always about how he feels. Did he show an ounce of concern for me or Christina when our mother died?

Fuck no. He sobbed and carried on, got drunk, disappeared for days at a time. I later learned he went to clubs. That's where he met Bambi, stepmama number one. Next was Candy. Who knew what was coming next?

He waves a hand at me as he turns into the back of the couch, clutching a pillow to his middle and heaving softly.

I despise him. And yet I still stand there for a long moment before I force myself to walk away.

I can't wait until I get to walk away forever.

CHAPTER
FIVE

Evie

"WELL, THAT LOOKED intense," Julie says as she comes over and sits on my bed with a Coke in her hand.

I take a sip of the Coke she poured over ice for me and nod. After Matt left, I listened to the sound of the car pipes until they faded away, then turned and went into the house. Julie was inside fixing drinks. Sarah had run into her room to play with her dolls.

"What are you doing here?" I ask. "And where's Mama?"

Today was usually her early day home from work.

"She got called back into the salon. Customer emergency or something."

I roll my eyes. "Do you mean Mrs. Hinch needs her roots touched up before her church ladies' social tonight?"

Julie laughs. "I don't know what it was, but Aunt Norma called and asked if I could watch Sarah since you weren't home yet."

Julie lives a block over from us, and I guess Mama decided not to wait for me to get home. I'm not all that late, but I should have called. The truth is that I didn't think of it. I'd have texted, but Mama didn't have a cell phone yet. I bought my own with money I earned working as a waitress because no way would Mama buy me one when she didn't have one herself. It wasn't a fancy phone, and I'm always careful since it's pay-as-you-go, but at least I have one.

Still, thank goodness Jules was home or I'd be in trouble.

"Okay, I answered your question," Julie says. "Now tell me what that was all about."

I sigh. "He's leaving. You were right."

Julie reaches out and squeezes my arm. "I'm sorry. When Jack told me, I didn't believe it either. Wow. I thought Matt was going to LSU. But West Point... didn't see that one coming."

"Me neither."

I still can't quite wrap my head around it. Since his mother died, Matt told me—when he talked about it—that he wanted to help people. I assumed he wanted to be a doctor. Search for a cure for cancer.

But the Army? I don't understand. It's people like me who join the Army—people who need money for college and don't have it—not people like Matt who can choose any college he wants and never pay a dime.

I'm still coming to terms with this, still trying to figure out what it means for Matt and me. As if there *is* a Matt and me.

There never will be now.

I pinch the bridge of my nose and work on breathing.

"He said we'll always be friends, that he'll stay in touch with me."

Julie sighs. "Well, that's something anyway. And he probably will. The two of you have been friends forever."

"I don't want to be friends." I clutch my fist to my chest where it hurts so badly. "I want him to feel what I feel, Jules. I want him to ache for me, to need me…"

My throat hurts. I can't tell anyone else this. But Jules understands.

"I know, Evie."

I close my eyes and roll my head around on my neck, easing the tension. "Three more weeks. He leaves right after graduation."

I still have another year to go before I graduate. I mean, I've always known I'll spend my senior year at Rochambeau High without Matt Girard—but I thought he'd be at LSU, close enough to come home on weekends. Close enough to visit if Mama lets me borrow the car sometimes.

He would realize someday what I already know—that we're meant to be together. I've always been certain of it and I'm willing to be patient.

But how is he going to do that if we never see each other anymore? What if he meets someone else? What if he forgets me?

I have to do something before I lose him forever. But I don't know what…

CHAPTER
SIX

Evie

"THERE'S A PARTY tonight," Julie says. "Out at Ro-chambeau Lake."

I look up to find her standing over me, grinning glee-fully. Her hair is pink today. She changes it about as often as other people change socks, so I don't even remark on it.

It's Friday and it's our lunch break. I didn't feel like eating in the cafeteria, so I grabbed my sack lunch and brought it outside where I could sit beneath one of the trees and think.

I want to be alone, but that's not really possible in high school, is it?

"So?" I say. I'm not in a party mood. Matt's leaving in two weeks and I don't know how to tell him what I feel. What I know about us deep inside.

"Soooo," Julie says, plopping down beside me and opening a pack of M&M's. "Everyone will be there. In-cluding Matt Girard, dumbass."

"How does that help me? The place will be packed." Which means that talking to Matt will be impossible. He's popular, and he's always the center of attention, especially with girls. Getting him alone at a thing like that? Not happening.

Not to mention, what the hell would I say? I love you, please love me too?

I shudder at the thought. Julie holds out the candy and I take a couple.

"So what if it is? Wear something sexy and talk to him. Get his attention. You don't have long left, babes."

We talked about this the other day. About what I need to do to let Matt know I want more from him. Be sexy was about all we came up with.

That and ask him to sleep with me. Be my first. I threw it out there as a last-ditch kind of solution, but the more I think about it, the more I like it.

Ask Matt to be my first. Ask him to initiate me, to take my virginity.

Oh, I like that thought a lot—but yeah, it scares the hell out of me too. How do I ask the guy who's been my best friend, who I played with in the mud when we were kids, to do something so outside the norm of our relationship?

Then again, if I don't ask him, how will he ever figure out that we're meant to be together?

Yeah, it's a real conundrum. Let things go on as they have been and wait anxiously to hear from him when he's away, or cross the line of our friendship and ask him outright to strip me naked and do all the things I've imagined doing with him?

It's easy to figure out which of those choices makes

my stomach twist into knots. I'm not saving myself out of some misguided idea that I have to remain pure until marriage. No, I'm saving myself for Matt. Always have been.

It isn't that I haven't tried to be with another guy. But when he slips a hand under my shirt and starts fondling my breasts, all I want is to get away. It doesn't feel right. It feels, well, disgusting.

"Come on, Eves. You can ride with Jack and me."

I look at her like she's lost her mind. "Ride with you and Jack? What about after, when he wants to take you parking?"

Parking being the euphemism for finding a field somewhere and fucking in the backseat. For once, I wish I was comfortable with that idea, that I'd done it before so it wasn't such a scary thought to approach Matt.

Julie shrugs. "We'll drop you back home first. No biggie."

I chew my lip. But how can I say no? It's one more chance to be near Matt, one more chance to talk to him. And maybe, just maybe, I'll get the courage to ask him to take me somewhere we can be alone.

"Okay, I'll go."

Julie bounces up and down. "Yay! Now come over to my house first. We'll get dressed together. I'll make sure you look your best. Matt won't know what hit him."

CHAPTER
SEVEN

Matt

I WASN'T PLANNING to go to the lake tonight, but the old man isn't home and I don't need to stay in that big lonely house and twiddle my thumbs while waiting for the next two weeks to go by.

All I have to do is keep out of trouble, but partying at the lake isn't going to be trouble. Yeah, there's drinking and pot smoking, but drinking isn't illegal—well, it is at my age but not as illegal as pot smoking, which I definitely won't do. No way am I fucking around with my appointment to the military academy.

I take my Vette and arrive around nine. The party is in the pavilion and the surrounding picnic areas. The Rochambeau PD can chase us out if there are complaints, but the park's open after dark. So long as we don't cause trouble, they won't have any reason to intervene.

The drinking is on the down low, of course. If the PD show up, they won't find any obvious alcohol—no beer cans or bottles. If they start handing out Breathalyzers, however, a lot of people will be screwed.

The trick is in not causing enough trouble to make that a reality.

I get out of my Vette and lock it, then head up to the pavilion. Jeanine spots me and sashays over with a big smile.

"Hey, Matt. Didn't think you were coming."

"Yet here I am."

She slips an arm around my neck and arches herself into me. I should put a stop to her blatant show of possession, but I don't much care at the moment. If she's willing to put out, that's good enough for me tonight.

I give her a quick kiss and set her away from me as I continue over to where some of the guys are standing around, drinking from cups with lids and straws. They look like simple gas station or fast-food-restaurant drinks, but I know there's whiskey mixed in there.

"Need a drink, bud?" Jimmy Thibodeaux asks.

Jimmy isn't one of my favorite people, but he's all right. Sort of cracked in the head sometimes, but still a good old boy.

"Whatcha got?"

"Old Charter and Coke."

"Sounds good to me."

Someone mixes a drink and hands it to me. I take a sip. Maybe I shouldn't do this. Maybe, considering how fucked up my father is, I should learn a lesson about drinking. But I'm seventeen, in control of myself. My father is fifty-three and a drunk.

I know the fancy word for it: *dipsomania*. So much more genteel than *alcoholism*. My father is a dipsomaniac, like a character in a William Faulkner novel. It fits, really, considering the house and the clichéd Southerness of my family.

But that doesn't mean I have a problem. I can sip this drink, get happy for a while, and then not worry about it again for a week. Next weekend is graduation, and I'm so getting trashed then. My last taste of freedom for a long time.

"Holy shit, who is that?" Jimmy asks, and I swing my head to look as two girls join some others at the edge of the pavilion.

I recognize Julie Breaux right away because she's in profile to me. Beside her, a tall girl in a skintight denim mini, sandals, and a red tank top has her back to me. Her hair is down to her ass, thick, dark, and curled at the ends.

Her ass looks amazing in that skirt, and her legs are so long they make my throat dry.

"I don't know," I say, taking a sip of my drink and starting toward the girls who are standing together off to one side of the pavilion. There are four or five of them, but I want to know who the one with her back to me is.

Julie nudges the girl as I approach, and she turns. I feel like someone knocked me in the head with a bat. I should have fucking known.

It's Evie—but Evie as I've tried so desperately not to see her. This is Evie as a *girl*. No, a woman—a beautiful woman with curves and a mouth I want to kiss.

Holy hell, Evie Baker isn't a tomboy anymore. I know that, of course. She was in my car just last week when we went out to the bayou. But she was wearing jeans and a T-shirt, not a frigging mini with her mile-long legs showing.

She has on makeup tonight, which isn't typical Evie. Red lips, long lashes, and the most gorgeous eyes I've ever seen. Her lips part and I keep walking. I hope like hell the shock doesn't show on my face.

"Hey," I say. "Didn't know you'd be here."

"Hey." She dips her gaze down to the ground for a second. Then she shrugs. "Sounded like fun."

When she meets my gaze again, my heart thumps. A feeling I don't quite recognize starts to swell in my chest. It's kind of like when I take some girl out and she wants to fuck and I want it too. That moment of blissful happiness where I know I'm getting laid and I want the release because it's pretty much the sweetest thing in my life, at least while it lasts.

Only this feeling is worse. Stronger. More desperate, because this is Evie and it isn't going to happen. Not with me—and not with anyone. I remember the look on Jimmy's face, and I know there is no way in hell I'm letting him get his hands on her.

I take her hand and she gasps in surprise. But I don't care as I tug her away from the girls and over to my car.

"Get in. I'm taking you home."

"What?" she asks. "No." She jerks her hand from mine and faces me, crossing her arms beneath her breasts.

Jesus.

"You shouldn't be here, Evie."

"And you should? What's the difference, Matt? I've been out here before, and you haven't said a damned thing about it."

She has been, but she didn't look like… well, this. Exciting and gorgeous and so damned appealing that every guy who sees her is getting a hard-on.

"It's almost graduation. These fuckers are crazy."

It isn't a good reason, but it's all I have. They *are* crazy. About to taste freedom and impatient to start the rest of their lives.

She nods to the cup in my hand. "And you aren't? You can't drive when you've been drinking."

I didn't even realize I'm still holding the cup. I throw it onto the grass. "I'm not drunk. I had one sip before you showed up."

"I'm not leaving, Matt. I just got here—and besides, why do you care? You're leaving Rochambeau. You won't even care what I'm doing then."

"I'll care," I say, my throat tight. "I'll always care."

CHAPTER EIGHT

Evie

MY HEART IS pounding. My skin is on fire. And my breathing is short and fast. I'm not scared. I'm excited.

Matt is looking at me like he's never seen me before. He's wearing jeans, flip-flops, and a faded tee that says Rochambeau Bulls on it. His eyes flash with heat, and his jaw clenches. He throws the cup away and stares me down with his chest rising and falling almost as fast as mine is.

His nostrils flare as if he's working to control himself. I have no idea what's going on with him, but it's like there is this electricity in the air between us.

"You aren't my boyfriend," I say. The words aren't easy to get out, especially since I have to say a word aloud that I've prayed for in secret.

Boyfriend.

I *want* Matt to be my boyfriend. I want Matt in my life, and I want more than he's ever given me before.

I went to Julie's house to get ready like she wanted,

and I gave her free rein. It isn't that I don't wear makeup or curl my hair—but I'm not as bold as she is. I don't work for fifteen minutes on the perfect cat eye or mascara my lashes into infinity. I don't spend time lining my lips and slicking on lipstick the way she does.

Maybe I should, because Matt is looking at me like he's never seen me before. It kind of pisses me off at the same time it thrills me.

"No, I'm your big brother," he says, and the anger welling inside me boils into a giant wave.

I take a step toward him, poking my finger in his chest. I've never done that before—or not since we grew up—and it feels good.

"You are *not* my brother, Matt. We aren't related at all. I'm just like all the other girls in school—"

His brows lower and he looks suddenly furious. "You are fucking *not* like the other girls—"

"I am! I like guys and I want a boyfriend of my own—I want some guy to want me, to take me on dates, to hold my hand and drive me in his car—"

"That's not all they want, Evie. You want romance and all that bullshit—guys want sex."

I lift my chin. My heart thumps. There is so much in that statement I can address. But there is only one thing I'm going to. "Maybe that's what I want too."

He takes a step closer then, his brows lowering even more. He looks pissed, and something about it thrills me more than it should.

"You're a virgin, Evie," he growls beneath his breath. "You need to save yourself for the right guy. A guy who cares about you and doesn't just want to get laid. A guy who'll treat you right."

Honestly, as fascinating as his anger is, it's also irritating. What a hypocrite. I know what he's been up to, what he's done with the girls he's taken out. Matt Girard is no virgin.

"Like you treat Jeanine and Tiffany and Bella and all the others, right?"

He grabs me again and this time he jerks me over to the passenger door and yanks it open. He's going to try to shove me in the car by force, but I'm having none of it.

If anyone is watching us, and I'm sure they are, they have to be as confused as I am. We must look like a couple having a fight. Yet we aren't a couple. We're friends.

I jerk free of his grip—not easy since Matt is bigger than I am and stronger—and stumble back a step.

"Don't you dare, Matt. Don't you fucking dare!"

His chest heaves as he stares at me. I have no idea what he might do next, but he turns and slaps his hand on top of the Vette explosively, swearing in Cajun French, which I do not speak, and English. I take a step back, awed and surprised by the force of his anger.

When he's through cussing, he slams the door and rakes a hand through his hair.

"Fine. Fucking fine—but don't you come crying to me when it all goes wrong, you got that? I tried."

I don't know what will happen next, what I should say, but I don't get the chance to figure it out. Matt strides away and leaves me standing beside his car. My heart hammers and tears prick at my eyes.

"Asshole," I hiss. And then I turn and go rejoin Jules and my friends.

CHAPTER
NINE

Matt

WHAT THE FUCK is wrong with me? I have no idea, but I can't take my eyes off Evie. I was fucking pissed when I left her standing beside my car. I went back to the pavilion, got another drink, and let Jeanine drape herself all over me.

I kissed her hard, shoved my tongue down her throat, and grabbed her ass when she rubbed up against me. She made a noise of approval deep in her throat, but it did nothing for me.

I pushed her away, gently, and hammered back that drink. Then I got another one. The whiskey was smooth and it soon took the edges off my irritation. I feel happier, freer. I can breathe again.

I watch Evie though because I can't stop. Jeanine tries to distract me, but it doesn't work. Eventually, she slips off to join her friends for a while, no doubt annoyed that she can't get me to take her away from here and have a quickie in her daddy's truck.

Oh yeah, she informed me she has his truck, complete with bench seat in the back. I'm not uninterested, but I can't drag myself away just yet.

Evie has a cup in her hand, but I don't know what's in it. She might be drinking, or not. Every once in a while our gazes meet. She tilts her chin up and gives me a cold stare. I don't like it.

Yeah, I fucked up by trying to force her into my car. I don't know what I was thinking except that I felt like I had to get her away from here. Home, where she'll be safe. Where Jimmy Thibodeaux and all the other guys can't touch her.

Touch her…

Jesus, she's a virgin, which I've resolutely tried not to think about after she told me. And tonight she said maybe she wants to change that. It makes me crazy to think of one of these assholes touching her. Taking advantage of her. Making her cry.

But, shit, she's sixteen and she *is* going to have sex with someone eventually. It's all part of growing up. If it isn't now or next year, it'll be in college with someone I won't even know.

I suck in a breath. Maybe that's better. I don't need to know who the guy is. I just need to know it isn't any of these assholes.

Why? Why do you need to know that?

Fuck, I don't know why. I suck down more of the whiskey and Coke. Yeah, I'm fucking insane. I blame it on my screwed-up life.

I let my gaze filter over the crowd. I know who I won't see here. Christina. My sister is shy, introverted. She doesn't do well in crowds. She prefers reading to socializing. If she has a crush on some guy, I don't know it.

She's in Baton Rouge this weekend, staying with our grandmother. She spends a lot of time there, but I never do. I mean, Grandmother is great and all that, but she's a lot like Christina—quiet, contained, happy with books and stuff. For me, a weekend with her is like watching paint dry.

Someone drags out speakers and starts playing music through a computer, a real deejay wannabe. The pumping beat gets people dancing, gyrating on the concrete floor. I watch it all with the kind of detachment I'd have watching monkeys at the zoo.

But then the music slows and people couple up. Jeanine comes over and runs a hand down my arm.

"Wanna dance?"

I'm not sure I answer, but she drags me onto the floor and wraps her arms around my waist. I put my arms around her but keep my drink. My head swims a little, but not too much.

"We should get out of here," Jeanine whispers in my ear. Or my collarbone, actually. She's standing on tiptoe, and she isn't tall enough to reach.

"In a bit," I say, warming up to the idea of getting some pussy tonight.

Fuck Evie anyway. Who does she think she is?

A pain in my ass, that's who she is. I'm only trying to help. Only trying to keep her from making a mistake.

She slides into my field of view then, standing in Jimmy's arms as they sway to the music. He's holding her close, but not as close as he wants. I can tell that from the way he keeps trying to bring her in and she keeps bracing her hands against him and refusing to cooperate.

Hell, they're practically touching pelvises already. What more does the asshole want?

And then he yanks her closer and she yelps. I see red. That fucking does it for me.

CHAPTER
TEN

Evie

I SHOULDN'T HAVE accepted Jimmy Thibodeaux's invitation to dance. But the music changed and he was there, holding out his hand and asking me for the slow dance. He's good-looking, though not as handsome as Matt. But maybe I need to move beyond Matt. Maybe I need to try to think about someone else for a change, see if that helps at all.

It definitely isn't helping. For one thing, Jimmy is all hands. He's been groping me since this dance started, his fingers sliding around to brush my breasts or down to my ass while he apologizes and pretends it's all a mistake.

But his grip on me is too strong and I can't break away. Jimmy is a linebacker for the Bulls, and he looks the part. Big, wide, powerful.

When he finally succeeds in jerking me closer to his body, I feel more than I want to feel. I've never been *this* close to a guy, but I'm pretty sure that bulge at his groin isn't a pistol.

On the other hand, Jimmy is a bit of a redneck. A pistol isn't out of the realm of possibility, though that sure is a strange place to keep it.

"Evie, you smell so good, look so good—what do you taste like?"

"Jimmy, no—" I try to twist away from the lips headed my way, but I'm not sure I'm going to make it.

And then Jimmy sails backward and I'm free. After trying so hard to jerk away from him, I have enough momentum to send me flying the other direction.

Someone catches my hand, and then I collide with a body.

"I got you. It's okay."

I look up into Matt's face, and my heart melts. Oh, I should be angry—I am angry—but he's holding me close. Really holding me close.

And it's everything I want.

His brows lower and he looks pissed. At me, at Jimmy, I have no idea. I brace for a fight with him, but all he does is tug me closer and tuck my head beneath his chin.

When he starts swaying to the music, I catch Julie's wide-eyed gaze. Her jaw has dropped open, and then she smiles and gives me a thumbs-up.

That's when I smell the whiskey. Matt is holding me, dancing with me in public, but he's also been drinking. And that means he isn't doing this with a clear mind.

But oh, what the hell, I don't much care. I'm dancing with Matt Girard. My body is plastered to his, his arms are around me, and his warmth flows into me.

He smells good and he feels like heaven. My heaven. I close my eyes and squeeze him tight. He squeezes back.

When I open my eyes again, Jeanine Jackson is standing on the edge of the floor, looking highly pissed off. I don't care. Jimmy is dancing with Susan Palmer, clearly having moved on now that Matt intervened.

The slow song doesn't last long enough. When it's over, Matt steps back and stares down at me. He looks like he's thinking about something, thinking hard, but I don't know what it can be.

"You grew up," he says.

"So did you."

He's frowning. Then he puts a hand in my hair and sifts his fingers through it, down to the ends. My scalp tingles with his touch.

"I miss you."

"I'm right here." My heart is in my throat as he continues to sift, sift, sift.

"No, I miss who you were. Who we were. My best friend. My Evie."

Oh, that hurts. It shouldn't, but it does. He misses us as kids. He misses the me who played in dirt and worshipped the ground he walked on, not the me I am now. I still worship the ground he walks on, but in a more realistic way.

Or so I hope.

"I'm not going to be that little girl ever again, Matt. We're here now, and this is what we are. You don't have to like it, but you can't change it."

"I won't be here to take care of you anymore. You have to be careful."

"How much have you had to drink?"

He shrugs. "Some. Not enough."

I take his hand and lead him off the dance floor and

over to a picnic table away from everyone. I make him sit down.

"You can't drive home this way. You have to sober up."

He catches my hand and presses it to his cheek. "Don't fucking care."

"You need to care. I think if you get a DWI, that's not going to go well with West Point."

Maybe it'll be the answer to my prayers if he suddenly can't go to West Point, but I don't want him to get in trouble for it to happen. That would be wrong. And I love him too much to want him hurt.

His gaze sharpens a little bit then. "No, you're right. Can't have that. Have to get away."

I sit beside him and slide my fingers along his cheek. He already put my hand there, so I feel like I can get away with it. He closes his eyes and groans.

"Matt... what's wrong? Why do you have to go away?"

"You wouldn't understand, Evie-girl."

"You can try me."

He squeezes his eyes tight, and then he opens them again and shakes his head. "No, *cher*."

No other excuse or explanation, just a flat-out no. I try not to let it bother me, but it does. This is the boy who cried on my shoulder when his mother died, and now he won't tell me something that is obviously causing him pain.

How far apart we've grown.

"Okay." I extract my hand and stand. "I'm going to go get you some water. Don't move."

"I won't." He grins and my heart turns over.

I hold my hand out. "Give me your keys."

He slides his fingers into his pocket and fishes them out, putting them in my palm without argument.

"Don't go anywhere," I repeat.

He leans back against the picnic table and crosses his legs at the ankles. "Not moving, baby. Promise."

I go to get water, then make my way back to where I left Matt. He's still there, which surprises me. I honestly expected he'd wander off somewhere the minute he was alone.

Except he isn't alone. Jeanine is there, straddling his lap, arms around his neck, mouth plastered to his. Ordinarily, I'd turn around and leave them alone, but not this time.

This time I'm ticked off and in full mama-bear mode. Matt doesn't need her tongue down his throat. He needs to sober up so he can drive home safely. I remember the keys in my hand then. Maybe *I* need to drive him home, make sure he gets there.

Alone.

I march over and slap the bottle of water down on the table. It's enough to make Jeanine jump. She turns glazed eyes to me, and I know she's about as drunk as Matt. Great.

"Get off him, Jeanine."

Matt grins up at me stupidly. "Hey, Evie-girl. Where'd you go?"

"Water." I twist the cap on the bottle and shove it at him. He takes it and slugs some back. Jeanine's still sitting on his lap, her lower lip thrust out in a pout.

"Go away, Evangeline. Nobody wants you here."

"Not true," Matt says.

"Honey," Jeanine says, turning back to him, "if she

stays, we can't be alone… and I need you alone. I need you so much."

I prop a hand on my hip and tell myself that committing violence against Jeanine probably won't be helpful.

"I'm sure he needs you too, Jeanine, but not right now. Matt's daddy called and he has to go home. Immediately. Family emergency."

Matt's gaze narrows, but he doesn't call me out on the lie. Jeanine's pout grows bigger, if possible. She turns to Matt, shutting me out.

"Baby, is that true?"

Matt shrugs. "Yeah, guess it is."

Jeanine tries to extract herself and ends up nearly falling on her ass. I save her, not Matt.

She jerks her arm out of my grip and steadies herself as she stands. "Call me later?"

"Absolutely," Matt says.

Jeanine toddles off toward the pavilion and Matt sucks down water.

"Do you have any taste at all?" I ask, exasperated. "You can do so much better."

He shrugs. "You got any suggestions?"

I do, but my tongue feels too thick to say the words. He's drunk and now is not the time.

We stare at each other for a long moment. Matt is still leaning back against the table, long legs sprawled in front of him, one arm spread along the table, the other bent as he clutches the water and takes swallows of it.

He looks like a decadent god lounging on his throne. I almost laugh at that idea, but it is kinda true. Maybe I read too many novels if I'm thinking like that. Thrones and gods, sheesh.

"So what's the emergency?" he asks.

"You know I made that up."

"Yeah, I know."

"I'm taking you home. You can't afford any trouble."

He climbs to his feet and sways a second. "Yeah, true."

He follows me toward his car, then stops when I click the button to unlock it.

"Wait... Can you even drive a stick?"

"Yes, I can. Uncle John taught me." Sort of, but I don't add that part. I've driven Uncle John's Chevy truck approximately three times. It's a column-shift—but it can't be all that different, right?

"Cool," Matt says. Then he gets into the Corvette and leans his head back on the seat, eyes closing.

I start the engine. Then I pray I make it home without damaging this fancy-ass car I could never afford to repair.

CHAPTER
ELEVEN

Matt

I'M CONFUSED WHEN I wake up. It's dark, but this isn't my bed. I sit up, and my mouth feels like a desert. I can use some water. My head is throbbing, but not badly. It's the Old Charter kicking in, of course, and I'm pissed that I had enough of that stuff to fuel a headache.

I'm still fully dressed. I swing my legs over the side of the bed and sit for a second. It takes a moment, but I start to make out objects in the room. Stuffed animals. A small dresser with a mirror. A lamp on the bedside table and a pile of books.

It occurs to me that the pleasant scent surrounding me is Evie's. I've been lying on her bed, my face in her pillow, breathing in her shampoo for who knows how many hours.

I shove myself to my feet and make my way from the tiny room and out into the hallway. There's a night-light glowing softly. I keep going until I reach the living room.

There's a form on the couch and I know it's Evie. She put me in her bed and took the couch. God knows what she told her mother. There was no need to tell the old man anything. He's at a strip club or a dive bar and unreachable, guarantee it.

"Evie," I croak because my throat is so dry.

She gets up instantly and comes to my side. Her fingers on my arm are cool. "Hey, you okay?"

"Yeah. Just need something to drink."

I need to piss too, but I don't tell her that. I know where the bathroom is. Hell, I know where the kitchen is. So why did I wake her?

Because I want to hear her voice again. Because I want her to be awake with me so I don't feel so alone.

"Come on," she says and leads me into the kitchen where she gets a glass, puts some ice in it, and adds tap water.

I take it and drink it down. She fills it again while I say, "Be right back."

She knows where I'm going. When I return, she's leaning against the sink, glass in hand. She gives it to me and I chug half of it. It's cool and crisp with a slight taste of chlorine or whatever it is they add to the water in Rochambeau.

"What did your mom say about this?"

"Not much. She agreed that bringing you here was better than taking you home. She called and left a message on the answering machine in case your dad comes home. Just said you were staying with us tonight. No mention of drinking."

I rake a hand through my hair. "Shit, did I get you in trouble, Evie?"

"No, I'm not in trouble. I didn't drink anything, and Mama believes I'm old enough to make my own choices. She also believes I'll make good ones, though I'm sure if I made a bad one, there would be consequences."

"She's pretty cool."

"She is. How do you feel?"

"Better now that I've had some water. But not great, no."

"Want something to eat?"

Actually, I am kind of hungry. But I have a feeling there are some things I shouldn't eat. Hamburgers. Greasy fried food. That sort of thing.

"Got anything easy on the stomach?"

"Cereal?"

"Sounds great."

"Sit down and I'll get it."

I sit at the small table near one window and Evie goes to work pulling out a bowl, a box of cereal, and some milk. Then she brings the bowl over to me and I thank her. I can tell it's Rice Krispies by the crackling sound.

She sits down and yawns, and I feel a prickle of guilt that I woke her. But the scent of her shampoo is still in my nose, and I'm glad she's here.

"Sorry about, you know, what happened at the party."

"Which part?" she says, and the guilt rises a little higher.

"All of it," I say, figuring that's the right answer. I remember that I tried to force her to leave, and then I remember dancing with her after shoving Jimmy away. I also remember letting Jeanine climb all over me and Evie chasing her off.

Shit, I *am* a jerk.

"It's okay," she says. "I ground the gears in your car and couldn't get out of third for about a mile. I figure we're even now."

I don't even care about the car, but yeah, it kinda shocks me that she's admitting that. I remember it now that I think about it. I wasn't that drunk. Well, okay, I was drunk and things are a little fuzzy, but I remember most of it.

"You said you could drive a stick."

"And I can. Just not very well it seems."

I want to laugh but I don't. "Why did you bring me to your house?"

"Because it's closer. If I drove you all the way out to Reynier's Retreat, I might have wrecked your engine or something. And even if I didn't, I'd have had to call Mama to come get me. Seemed easier to come here."

I can't fault that logic. Plus I'm glad we're here. There's something sweet and simple about Evie's house. It's small, but it's more of a home than Reynier's Retreat can ever be.

I reach for her hand. She doesn't pull away from me, and that makes me happy. Content. "Thanks for looking out for me."

"I know how much going to West Point means to you. If you got pulled over while drinking... Well, I think that might be a problem."

I squeeze her hand. Fucking hell, I adore this girl. She really is the best friend I've ever had, and I'm kind of sorry I spent the past few years pushing her away.

I had to do it though. She's been growing up, growing pretty, and I didn't want to ruin our friendship by preying on her feelings for me. Because that's the kind of asshole

I'm capable of being.

And then there's Candy and my stupidity of falling for her. No one knows about that, but if Evie and I were still close, I might have told her just to have someone to talk to.

I'm pretty sure that's not a good idea. What would she think of me if she knew?

"You're the best, Evie-girl. I owe you."

She pushes her long hair back over one shoulder and sighs. "Keep your promise to stay in touch with me when you're gone. That's the only thing you owe me."

I will. Of course I will. How can I ever forget Evie?

CHAPTER
TWELVE

Evie

"WAIT A MINUTE… He didn't even try to kiss you?"

I shake my head as Julie stares at me in disbelief. It's Monday and we're on our way to school in Julie's old Chevy. We're at a stoplight and she's grilling me about the party and what happened after Matt and I left.

"He was drunk, Jules. I took him home and put him to bed."

"Oh for fuck's sake, Evie. He would have kissed you if you'd encouraged him! He was looking at you like you were a giant chocolate cake. He couldn't keep his eyes off you! And when he threw Jimmy across the floor? Whoa, I thought for sure that was it."

My ears are red. Yeah, it all sounds awesome, but it just didn't pan out that way. Which means Matt hadn't really been looking at me like I was cake. More like I was his little sister who needed saving. He pulled Jimmy off me the same as he would have done if it had been Christina.

He wouldn't have danced with Christina after that, but so what? It wasn't much different, really. I was his friend. His little sister in his eyes. That was the extent of it.

He'd been drunk, kissing Jeanine like she was made of the whiskey he'd been drinking and wanted more of, and yet he'd never tried to kiss me. Not once.

Yeah, that really makes me feel special. Even drunk he wouldn't touch me. How can I ask him to be my first after that?

"Well, it wasn't. Matt's not interested in me."

The light turns green and Julie presses the gas. "Could have fooled me. Could have fooled a lot of people actually. I thought Jeanine was going to lose her shit when Matt started dancing with you."

I recall the look on Jeanine's face when I told her to get lost. Yeah, if Jeanine remembers that, it's not going to be a great day at school.

Thankfully Jeanine's a senior, which means this week is the last I have to be around her on a daily basis.

I sigh. Holy crap, I had Matt Girard in my house, in my bed, and he still hadn't attempted to kiss me or anything. He held my hand and wouldn't let go while he ate his cereal, but that was it.

He confused me and frustrated me. Just when I thought there might be something more, that I wasn't the only one who felt all this crazy-hard emotion, he left me more baffled than ever.

"It's not over yet," Julie says. "You still have another chance."

My heart thumps. "He's not into me, Jules."

"Fuck that, yes he is. He just won't admit it to himself."

I lean back and close my eyes, rubbing my fingers against my temples. "Maybe in a year, when he comes home on break or something, he'll be ready to see me differently because he'll have been away."

"And what if he meets someone in college, huh? What if he comes back engaged or something?"

Okay, now that thought feels as if someone jabbed me in the gut with a sharp, hot knife. It's still sizzling and smoking, and I'm dying inside.

"He's not going to meet someone in a year."

I don't really know that, of course, but I have to say it, as if speaking the words is an incantation.

"There's a party Friday night, out at Billy Davis's hunting cabin. Everyone will be there. It's the last big blowout before Matt goes away."

I know where the cabin is because I've been there before. It's on a dirt road in the middle of the woods. The bayou isn't far, but far enough that the gators won't come sneaking up to the house.

"He might not go. He doesn't want to get in trouble before he leaves."

Julie snorts. "He'll go. He can crash there if he gets wasted. Everyone can. It's your last chance, Evie. Kiss him or bang him, I don't care—but do *something.*"

I don't know what I'm going to do. When we talked about asking Matt to be my first, it seemed like a great idea—but it was abstract, not a real plan in the sense that I know precisely what to say and what to do.

I have no idea what to say. When I asked Julie, she laughed and told me to tell Matt I want to fuck him and that would be enough to get the ball rolling.

Well, yeah, I'm sure it would. I just don't know if I can say it like that. Or if he'll laugh at me—or, worse, be disgusted—if I do.

"At least get him alone and kiss him. If he doesn't jump you, then you have your answer."

She's right about that. "Fine, I'll go."

"Good." Julie makes the turn into Rochambeau High and stops in the student parking lot. Then she looks at me. "You're going to have to up your game, Evie. Don't hint. Kiss him if he doesn't kiss you first. Tell him what you feel. Make sure there's no way he doesn't know."

I've been thinking about this all weekend and I know she's right. I don't know when or if I'll get another chance to be alone with Matt, but at some point, if it happens...

Well, I just have to be the one who makes the first move.

CHAPTER THIRTEEN

Matt

AFTER THAT NIGHT at Evie's house, I try to get back to normal. I take Jeanine out Wednesday night. And yeah, I definitely have a good time. She's soft and warm, so wet and ready for me. I hesitate right before plunging into her body, as if it's wrong somehow.

But it's dark and I can pretend she's someone else. I know exactly who I'm going to pretend she is. While it horrifies me in one sense, it turns me on wildly in another. I come hard and then I take her home.

What the fuck is wrong with me? That's what I don't understand. Why, after all these years, is it Evie's face I see when I fuck Jeanine? And why does that make me lose my mind?

I don't know, and I'm not going to find out. Graduation is Thursday night. One more week and I'm gone, off to prepare for the start of my new life. I could have stayed in Rochambeau for a little while longer, but I've arranged everything to leave immediately. I have to report to West Point in early July. For the three weeks before that, I'm staying with family friends in DC and New York.

I can't wait.

The old man isn't around much. He's on a drinking spree lately, spending his time at the clubs and ignoring Christina and me. If not for the housekeeper and cook, we'd have to take care of ourselves. Not that it's a hard thing to do, but when you have a parent, isn't he supposed to be involved in your life and care whether or not you eat McDonald's for every meal or have something home cooked?

Christina reads her books and shrugs. I worry about her being here for the next year without me, but Christina never makes the old man mad the way I do. He never slaps her, not ever.

But what if that changes when I leave?

My stomach aches as I think of it. All the things I haven't considered while I've been determined to get the hell out of here. What will happen to Christina? What will happen to Evie?

It's too late to worry about it now. If I wash out of West Point, I have to come back here and endure my father's weaknesses, his rages, his attempts to control me.

And he will control me, because he has the money. Until I reach the age of twenty-five and gain control of my trust, I'll be doing whatever the fuck my old man wants me to do.

I'm determined that isn't going to happen.

Graduation day comes and I walk across the stage. If my father is there, I don't know it. But Mrs. Doucet is there. She's the Girard family lawyer and has been for ages. So is Mrs. Simpson, our housekeeper, and Bonnie, the cook. They clap and cheer for me, and I salute them with a tip of my fingers at my cap as I walk across the stage.

After the ceremony, I spot Evie talking to Mrs. Simpson. She turns at my approach and then runs over and gives me a huge hug. Evie's mama and little sister are there too. It touches me more than I can say.

"Congratulations, Matt," Evie says, her eyes sparkling. "You must be so excited."

She flips the ends of the honor cords that hang around my neck. I worked hard for those, and I think some people are surprised to see me with them. But they're mine, earned legitimately. I've always known that the way I get to choose what I want out of life is to do well in school. Sure, the old man's money would get me into college—but I want more than to be in his debt.

That's why it has to be one of the military academies. Financial need has nothing to do with getting a full ride. The only "person" I'll owe anything to after West Point is the United States.

"Thanks, *cher*," I say. "I didn't know you'd be here."

Evie turns to her mother and sister. "We wouldn't have missed it, would we?"

Ms. Breaux—she changed her name back to her maiden name after her last divorce, which is why her name is different from Evie's—comes over and hugs me. Sarah clings to my leg and tugs on my gown. I ruffle her hair.

"'Gratulations, Matt," Sarah says. And then she smiles a gap-toothed smile before running off to do or see something.

Ms. Breaux smiles and says "Sorry" before running after Sarah. Evie is still here, still smiling up at me.

"Happy for you, Matt," she says.

I have the most insane urge to kiss her as she stands there, looking so sweet and hot and pretty.

"Can't believe it's here," I say, and that is true. You spend all your life wanting to graduate, and then you do. But there's so much left to do and see that I can't wrap my head around it. So much life left to live, if I'm lucky.

Evie's eyes sparkle. "Nowhere to go but up."

"Yeah." I put my arm around her and pull her into my side. It feels right.

Christina appears then, smiling and looking pretty in her blue dress and heels. She's shy, my sister, but the sweetest person I know.

"Matt," she says, and I let go of Evie and hug Christina hard. Goddammit, my eyes are watering.

"Chris," I breathe. "Next year's your turn, honey."

"Can't wait," she says, and I know it's true. In her own way, she wants to leave every bit as much as I do.

But Christina actually has Girard Oil in her blood. I'll be surprised if she isn't the CEO in ten years. My sister is the Girard who's going to take the company to new heights, not me. My father doesn't know that yet, but he will eventually.

"Proud of you, Mattie."

"Thanks, sweetie."

I don't remember everything that happened next. Lots of congratulations from teachers and friends, and a lot of high fives and shit with my classmates. We have a good time.

And then it's over and everyone's driving away. There are parties—of course there are parties—and I hit a few of them. But there is no one there I want to see, and I end up going home earlier than I planned to.

I lie in bed, alone, and stare up at the ceiling. It was supposed to be a great night, and yet I feel empty. Emptier than I ever have before, because everything I've worked for is finally here. Yeah, I have to make it at West Point—I can't wash out and get sent home—but I'm not really worried about that. I've dealt with the old man long enough that nothing about the military scares me.

Sure, maybe he collapses and falls apart after his rages, but his psychological warfare is top-notch. He never surrenders there. Never.

I close my eyes but sleep won't come. I had a beer or two, but not enough to affect me. I throw back the covers and prowl downstairs. The house is quiet. Christina is in her room, reading or asleep, and our father is still not home.

I go into the study. I open my father's liquor cabinet and take out a bottle of whiskey. He might notice it's gone, he might not. I don't much fucking care.

I take it back upstairs and slug it straight from the bottle. I don't want to get wasted. I just want to sleep. It takes a few pulls before the alcohol hits my system and makes me mellow.

I'm not trying to think about anything in particular, but before I know what I'm doing, I pick up my phone and dial a number I got by stealing it from her phone while she washed up my cereal bowl. It takes a few rings, but she answers.

"Hello?"

"Hey, Evie. Whatcha doing?"

"Matt? What's wrong?"

"Nothing. Can't sleep."

"Me either…" I don't believe her because she sounds sleepy. "Hey, how'd you get my number?" she asks.

"I programmed it in the other night at your house."

"Oh. I would have given it to you if you'd asked."

"Just as easy to take it off the phone."

"I guess so… Can't believe I won't see you in the halls next year," she says softly.

I can hear the sadness in her voice. I wanted to graduate, wanted to go, but now it's kind of scary too. It's here, it's real, and there's no going back.

"Yeah, it's kinda weird. But after next year, you'll be done. Then you'll go off to college somewhere too."

As soon as I say it, I wonder if I've said the wrong thing. I know Evie's mother doesn't have a lot of money. There's no guarantee that Evie is going to college. She might stay in Rochambeau and get a job. Or maybe she'll learn to be a hairdresser and work with her mother. Then again, I expect she'll do something with food. She's been interested in recipes and flavors for as long as I can remember.

"I suppose so. Still have to put up with Mrs. Watson's English class next year. She has it in for me."

I laugh. "She has it in for everybody… Hey, you going to Billy Davis's tomorrow night?"

"That's the plan."

"Then I'll see you there."

I can hear her yawn. "Yep, see you then."

"Night, Evie."

"Night."

I end the call and sit in the dark, staring at nothing. Then I pick up the whiskey bottle and take another swig. I need to fill this emptiness inside, at least for a little while.

CHAPTER FOURTEEN

Evie

I'M NERVOUS. I change clothes three times, finally settling on a silky pink tank top with a lace hem and a pair of low-rise jeans that are artfully ripped and flare over the flat sandals I'm wearing.

Maybe I should wear a skirt, but by the time I think about changing again, Julie is here, waiting for me to get in the car and go.

"Y'all be careful," Mama says, frowning a bit as she looks at us. Julie's boyfriend, Jack, is here too, dutifully standing with his hands clasped. Coming inside is points for him, so that's good.

But yeah, here we are, three teenagers getting ready to drive off into the sunset. Well not quite, as it isn't dark yet, but it will be in another hour.

"We will, Mama," I say, kissing her before we turn and go down the steps and get into Jack's car.

I told her we were going to the lake, but really we're

going to Billy's. The lake is a popular spot to hang out and the police patrol there. But a hunting cabin in the woods? Mama probably would put the brakes on that particular plan.

I have my cell phone and Mama can call me, so I don't worry she'll go looking for me. Besides, there are people at the lake, no doubt. The ones who weren't invited to Billy's, the geeks and underclassmen and wannabes.

I hate lying about where I'm going, but I have to see Matt tonight. He has one week left, and I'm not going to lose my chance to let him know we can be so much more to each other if only he'll give in to it. I'm more convinced of that than ever after last night.

I keep thinking of how I was startled awake, how I picked up the phone and answered it because the display said it was Matt—he must have programmed his number into my phone when he took mine—and how I thought I was dreaming at first. But no, it was really Matt. And he wanted to know if I would be at Billy's tonight.

Does it mean anything? Or not? I have no idea. I told Julie about it earlier this afternoon when she came by. She gave me a thumbs-up and a huge smile.

"He wants you, Evie. Trust me."

I wish I could believe her, but who can tell with Matt? If I were any other girl in his life, yeah, I'd probably agree. But I wasn't. Our relationship is different—and I don't know if he called me because he was lonely and needed a friend, or if he was thinking about me the way he thought about other girls.

"Omigod," Julie says as we hit the road. "Can you believe we're seniors now?"

She's excited as she takes a cigarette from Jack and

fires it up. I haven't thought much about it, but yeah, we're the seniors now. Julie cracks the window open and blows the smoke out. I don't smoke so I'm grateful. I don't like the smell.

My heart trips along the closer we get to the road leading to Billy's. I don't know what I'm going to do when I see Matt. Play it cool, I suppose.

A prickle of dread slides down my spine. What if he doesn't come? What if he changes his mind?

Don't borrow trouble. That's a phrase Mama likes to say, so I repeat it to myself now. If he doesn't show up, I'll deal with it then—and I'll think of a backup plan.

When we pull into the grass near the cabin, there are people outside on the porch and a grill going a little ways from the house, smoke rising into the trees. I scan the cars for Matt's Corvette, but it isn't there. My stomach knots as I get out of Jack's car and shut the door. The smell of grilling meat permeates the air, but I'm not hungry. I'm too nervous to be hungry.

I left my hair down, and I push it back over my shoulders. It's hot out here, and for a minute I wish I'd put it into a ponytail, but I didn't because I thought of Matt sifting his fingers through it last weekend. My entire scalp tingled with every stroke, and my heart tripped along like a race car.

Julie takes Jack's hand and we walk up to the cabin. Billy Davis calls out when he sees us. Someone else asks if we want a beer. Julie and Jack accept. I hesitate, then take one. I might need some courage if Matt shows up.

Jeanine Jackson's gaze is frosty when I walk inside the cabin. It's one big room, open concept, and she's standing by the kitchen island, leaning over it with her cleavage hanging out. But Matt isn't here.

I'm glad for it since I don't want to compete with Jeanine for his attention. He's chosen me over her twice now, but that doesn't give me much confidence because it's been for specific reasons each time—neither of them romantic.

Missy Sue LeBlanc comes over, smiling. "Hey, Evie, how's it going?"

"Great. You?"

Missy Sue leans toward me. "Fricking awesome. School's out and I'm going to party and shop and sleep in for the next three months!"

I laugh. Clearly, Missy Sue is already on her second or third wine cooler of the evening. "Sounds like a plan."

"You bet your ass it is."

Jason Harper comes over and slings his arm around Missy Sue's neck. "Hey, babe."

Missy Sue throws her arms around Jason's neck and kisses him. I take the opportunity to escape. I sip my beer as I wander through the room. Eventually, I ditch it and grab a Coke instead.

Julie calls me over to where a group of girls are sitting together. I perch on the arm of the chair and join in the conversation. A couple of the girls are seniors who just graduated, but most of us are juniors looking forward to what next year will bring.

Our last homecoming. Last prom. Last year at Rochambeau High. Then it's on to college for some. Others are looking forward to getting jobs and finally living on their own, making their own decisions.

Considering where I live and how much Mama struggles to make ends meet for the three of us, I know that moving out and having a job isn't necessarily going to give these girls the freedom they're so sure waits on the other end of high school.

I know where I want to go, but I haven't told anyone. I haven't even told Mama. I want to go to the Culinary Institute of America and learn how to be a chef. I love cooking, love experimenting with food. I learned a lot working with Charlie out at the diner last summer, and I'm planning to work there again this summer.

He's the one who told me about the Culinary Institute of America and how awesome it would be to graduate from there. Affording it is a different matter, which is why I haven't said anything to Mama. She wants me to live at home and attend the community college for two years.

And who knows, that might be exactly how it turns out. I don't really have a plan, other than applying for scholarships. But now I know I want the New York campus since it will at least be in the same state as West Point.

Julie finishes her beer and goes for another. Billy and a couple of the other guys bring in hamburgers and hot dogs, and several of the girls drift over to the kitchen island to fix something to eat. I sip my Coke and watch the door. The sun slips behind the trees, casting everything in an orange glow before winking out and leaving darkness behind.

Chris Frye arrives with his computer and speakers and starts deejaying in one corner. More people arrive, eventually spilling out of the house, onto the porch, and down into the yard.

I look at my phone. It's after nine and Matt still isn't here. Maybe he isn't coming after all. But then another pair of headlights appears in the long drive and my hopes lift.

It isn't a Corvette though. Julie appears a second later, looking excited. She's had at least two beers by now, maybe three.

"It's him," she says. "It's Matt."

My heart kicks up. "Where?"

"He just got here. He's driving his daddy's Escalade."

And, boom, my evening changes. I go from disappointed to elated and terrified all at once.

Maybe I need a drink after all.

CHAPTER FIFTEEN

Matt

THE OLD MAN came home tonight. I was getting ready to go out when he staggered in with a giggling bimbo who clearly came from a strip club. Gotta hand it to the dude, he knows what he likes.

They fell on the couch in the family room, giggling and kissing. When I walk in to see what the racket is, the woman—a bleached blonde with fake tits and a spray tan—glances up. Her eyes widen as she stares at me like I'm a gazelle and she's a starved lioness.

"Who's this?" she purrs.

My father peers around her. "My son," he says. And then he adds, as if seeing where this is going, "He's a prissy little faggot."

I'm not, but what's the sense in arguing?

"Too bad," stripper woman says. "He's cute."

"Get us a drink, boy," the old man says. "Make it a double."

I seethe the whole time but I go over to the sideboard like a good Southern gentleman and fix two bourbons in highball glasses. Then I walk over and set them on the coffee table. The old man grabs his and hammers about half of it back.

The woman makes a show of daintily sipping hers while eyeing me. "Too bad," she murmurs. "Too, too bad."

"Is there anything else you need?" I ask. So fucking polite. It's a wonder I don't explode with all the rage I feel inside.

"Where's your sister?"

"I think she's with Grandma, sir."

I know Christina drove to Baton Rouge. She probably won't come back for days. Who the hell could blame her?

The old man swings his head to look at the stripper, who's batting her eyelashes and acting dainty. "You ready to party, sweetheart?"

"Oh, Beauregard, you know it."

Jesus.

The old man looks at me. "Go on and get the fuck out, boy. Don't come back tonight."

"Yes, sir." As if I intend to.

I hesitate at the door, but then I pick up the keys to his Escalade. My father can't drive a stick shift, so I leave the Corvette and take his Caddy. Maybe I should have left it there, hoping he got a wild hair and drove off into the bayou tonight, but the truth is I don't hate him that much.

I definitely hate him, but if he fucking killed himself in a drunken wreck, then everything I've planned will get fucked up as Christina and I go into limbo while the estate is settled.

Nope, not happening. I take the Escalade and drive out to Billy Davis's place, breathing easier the entire way. One week, I remind myself. One fucking week.

It's after dark when I arrive, and the party is in full swing. I get out of the Escalade and let the sound of laughing voices trickle down like a soft rain. My heart still hurts, but I know this will help me feel better. I just need a few drinks, a soft girl in my arms, and I'll be set.

I'll spend the night here, so drinking isn't a worry. Not everyone will because of parents, but some of us— those with parents who don't give a shit, the ones who are eighteen, the ones who've told the perfect lies about why they aren't coming home—will stay the whole night and maybe into the next.

I stride toward the house and a chorus of cheers goes up when I step into the light. The old man might not be happy to see me, but these people are.

"Fucking A, Matt Girard's here," someone says. Someone else pushes a beer into my hand.

"Now this party's getting started!"

"Who's got the weed?"

"Light that doobie up."

"None for me," I say, holding up a hand.

I haven't smoked pot in two years now, not since I knew I wanted to go to West Point. I'm not taking any chances.

I pass inside where the noise level is higher than outside. Half the senior class is here, and a lot of the juniors as well. I search for the one junior I want to see, even while I tell myself I don't need to go there.

I don't know why I called her last night, except that hers was the voice I most wanted to hear. After we hung up, I drank a little more whiskey and then fell asleep. It wasn't long after we hung up, either. I don't know if hearing her voice helped me sleep, or if I was finally just tired enough to let it happen.

"Hey, baby." Jeanine put a hand on my arm. She's no doubt thinking we're a thing again since I fucked her the other night. But that ship definitely sailed a long time ago. I dated her for three months, we broke up, got back together for another month, and then broke up again.

It didn't help that I was dating her right after the Candy crisis. I'd have dated anyone who spread her legs for me as regularly as Jeanine did, no matter how much drama and maintenance went along with the deal.

"Hey, Jeannie."

"I'm so glad you made it tonight. Been thinking about you since the other night."

She dips her eyelashes down shyly, but it's all a ruse because Jeanine isn't shy.

"*Cher*," I say, "I'm glad you had a good time. But you know this isn't going anywhere, right?"

She blinks at me. I don't think she expected that, though she should. I'm fucking leaving and I've made that pretty clear to everyone and anyone who will listen.

"I never said I wanted it to." Her voice is prissy and I know she's lying. Maybe she thinks we'll have a long-distance romance when I'm gone, or maybe she thinks I'll change my mind about going.

Not happening.

I smile at her as if I take her words at face value. "That's good, baby, because I'm not coming back for a long time."

I don't know what she says after that because I suddenly spot a tall, dark-haired girl across the room. Someone moved and revealed her standing there, like the parting of the Red Sea or something. She's in profile to me, her long hair hanging down to her ass, her breasts curving out from her body. She's wearing a silky-looking top with tiny straps and low-slung jeans that hug her hips.

I don't know if someone nudges her or if it just happens, but she turns her head and our eyes meet. I feel a jolt down into my groin. I don't know what she feels, but suddenly she breaks eye contact and slams back the drink she's holding.

Then she sets the cup down and starts walking toward me.

CHAPTER
SIXTEEN

Evie

COURAGE. THAT'S WHAT'S in the cup. The second Julie tells me Matt is here, I go straight over to the bar and pour a shot of Jack Daniel's into a red Solo cup. I don't know what I'm going to do with it since I don't even like whiskey, but the second I see Matt, I slam it back.

My eyes are watering and I want like hell to cough, but I manage not to do it. The whiskey burns its way into my stomach and sends fire through my veins. It also dulls the edges of my fear.

I can't believe I'm going to do this, but I am. I thought about working my way up to it, talking to Matt, waiting for the right moment. But I know me and there will never be a right moment. I just have to say it.

And if I'm going to say it, I need courage. That's what the whiskey is for. Damn, but that stuff burns.

Matt watches me approach. He isn't alone, but that doesn't stop me. I see Jeanine walk away, which fills me with giddiness. Some of the guys are there with him, but he isn't paying any attention to them. He's watching me.

"Hi, Matt," I say when I reach him.

"Hey, *cher*."

"I started to think you weren't coming tonight."

His eyes seem haunted for a moment. "Had a delay. It's all good now."

Then he smiles and a warm feeling fills me. Damn, I love his smile.

"I want to ask you something," I say, my heart beating a million miles an hour. *Now or never, girlie. Got to do it. He's the one. The ONE.*

"Sure, ask away."

I glance at the guys standing near. They aren't listening to us, or even watching us, but that doesn't mean I'm going to blurt it out. Oh God, my stomach is roiling and my heart is beating so fast I think I might pass out. But I don't. I swallow. Hard.

Then I step closer to Matt and stand on tiptoe. I'm tall, but he's taller. He smells good, some sort of subtle male scent I can't identify. No overwhelming masculine body sprays or shit for him.

He tips his head toward me, listening.

I close my eyes.

"I want you to be my first."

There, I said it. Maybe not the best way I can, but he knows what I'm talking about. He knows I'm a virgin.

I lower myself and step back. He's looking at me so fiercely I think I should turn and run. But I don't. I just stand there, staring back.

He reaches for my hand, clasps it in his. And then he leads me out the door and down the steps. I don't ask where we're going. I don't dare speak. I follow him to the Escalade.

He opens the passenger door, but instead of letting me get inside, he backs me up against the seat, his body penning me in. His arms are on either side of me, trapping me. I gaze up at him, unsure where this is going, still scared half to death and certain I crossed a line I can never retreat back to.

And then he takes a step closer, his body pressing up against mine. He's warm, solid, and I shiver with excitement. One hand comes up, and then his fingers are on my cheek, sliding into my hair, cupping my head.

"Evie," he says, his voice soft.

I put my hands on his chest, surprised to find his heart beating fast too. How can Matt be nervous?

"Kiss me," I blurt. Because I'm afraid this is going to end, that he'll step away any moment or lecture me about waiting for the right guy.

He stands there, looking like he's warring with himself, and my heart sinks to my toes. I've done it now. I've gone too far. At least, thank God, he's leaving town next week and the humiliation will have time to blow over.

"Fuck," he whispers. And then he cups my cheeks in both his hands and lowers his head.

When his mouth touches mine, I'm so surprised I gasp—and that gives him the opportunity to slip his tongue into my mouth.

Oh my God, it's heaven. Everything I've ever wanted. Ever needed. He's giving it to me right now, years' worth of fantasies and dreams.

My fingers curl into his shirt as his mouth continues to taste mine. I've been kissed, of course I have, but not like this. Not where I think my heart is going to burst from my chest or that I'll die of happiness right here and now.

His hands slip from my face, down my shoulders, around my body. He pulls me in tight and kisses me like I've never been kissed before. It's everything I've imagined and more.

When he finally stops, when he gently takes me by the shoulders and sets me away from him, I'm woozy. Drunk on his kiss. Stone in love with this boy. I will do anything for him right this minute. Anything at all.

"Get in the car, Evie," he says tightly.

I obey without question. He goes around and gets in the driver's side. Then he starts the car without a word and backs up so he can turn around and start down the long drive.

I have no idea where we're going or what will happen now. But I know that everything between us has changed.

Forever.

CHAPTER SEVENTEEN

Matt

NO WAY IN hell am I taking Evie's virginity. When she sashayed up to me with those sweet hips swinging and a soft smile on her face, I was mesmerized.

When she stood on tiptoe to whisper in my ear, I smelled the hint of whiskey on her breath. And then she whispered the words that rocked my world.

I want you to be my first…

I got hard immediately. I wanted, more than anything, to kiss her. Instead, I took her hand and led her to the car, intent on putting her in it and taking her home. Straight home. No way did Evie need to be at that party, drinking shots and asking guys to be her first.

A part of my brain told me she wasn't going to ask anyone else, that it was something she wanted me—and only me—to do.

Goddammit, I can't do that to her. I can't take what she so sweetly offered.

Why not?

Someone's going to be her first, why not me?

No.

If I hadn't gotten weak and kissed her before putting her in the SUV, I wouldn't be thinking like this. But I *had* kissed her…

And holy fuck, what a kiss it was. Her tongue against mine, our breaths mingling—it feels different with Evie than it does with anyone else. I don't know why. Or maybe I do.

Maybe it's our history and this sudden change from best friends to sizzling attraction.

"Where are we going?" she asks, and I glance over at her.

My heart skips a beat. "I'm taking you home."

She doesn't say anything at first. And then she crosses her arms. "Take me back to the party."

"No. You need to go home, Evie."

"Don't you fucking dare," she spits out. "You don't get to tell me what to do. It's not your call. If you don't want to be my first, then take me back to the damn party. I'll find someone else."

My stomach clenches tight at those words. I flip on the blinker and whip onto a road that I know leads into a field where I can park the Escalade and no one will bother us. I don't mean to do it. I really don't.

But now I'm driving down a dirt lane, between the farmer's crops, until I reach the clearing I'm looking for. I put the Escalade in park and sit there with both hands on the wheel. Arguing with myself.

What am I doing? Why am I here? This is Evie, little Evie, and I need to take her home right now.

"Am I that ugly?" Her voice is whisper-soft, near to breaking.

I look at her, at those beautiful eyes in that beautiful face, and I feel something snap inside me.

"You aren't ugly, Evie. You're perfect."

She snorts. "Says the guy who won't take what I want to give."

I reach over and tuck her hair behind her ear. I shouldn't touch her, but I need to.

"Is this really what you want?"

Her eyes sparkle with unshed tears as our gazes meet. She sucks in a breath, heaves it out. "Would I ask you if I didn't? I trust you to do it right."

Oh sweet Jesus.

"Do you understand what you're asking?"

She clasps my hand and presses it to the underside of her breast. It's soft and round and my dick gets hard again.

"I think I get what this entails," she whispers.

Oh Lord, fuck me, I'm doomed. What am I doing? But I can't stop touching her. I don't want to stop touching her. Something about being with Evie makes me feel good, and I don't want that to end. Asking me to quit is like asking me to stop a boulder from crashing down a mountain after it's already rolling.

I reach over and drag her across the console, fusing my mouth to hers. She tangles her fingers in my hair and kisses me back, our tongues sliding together over and over again.

I don't know how long we kiss, but it's a long time. I'm hard, so damn hard, but kissing her is sweet. Part of me is dumfounded at this turn of events.

This is Evie, my Evie, my friend. And I'm planning

to strip her naked and use her body the same way I used Jeanine and Tiffany and all the others.

My conscience pricks me now and again, but I rationalize what I'm doing by telling myself if it isn't me, it will be someone else.

I don't want it to be someone else. I want it to be me. I can make it good for her, make her first time special.

And, yeah, it's totally selfish of me to justify myself this way. But I do. Why shouldn't I be the one? Why shouldn't I take what she's offering me?

I slip my hands beneath her top and run my palms up her silky sides. She shudders. I drag her shirt up, breaking the kiss long enough to slip it over her head.

I drop it on the passenger seat and reach for her bra as I find her mouth again. My fingers tangle in her bra strap, and I unsnap it on one try.

I feel her flinch, but then I gently pull it from her shoulders and drop it. When I break the kiss to look at her hovering over me, I feel a jolt all the way to my toes.

Fuck, she's gorgeous. Her breasts aren't small, but they aren't huge. The nipples are tightly beaded, upturned, and I cup her breasts gently, sliding my thumbs over her nipples.

She gasps and bites her lip, tilting her head back and thrusting her breasts toward me. What comes next is obvious to me. I lick a nipple and Evie moans. The sound is like a whip to my need, spurring me on.

But this isn't how I want to do this. I wish we had a bed, but we don't. We do, however, have a backseat. I want to lie on top of her, suck her nipples and taste her pussy, before I thrust my cock into her body.

Sitting up is becoming more uncomfortable as my

dick grows harder and my jeans don't stretch to provide more room.

"Evie, honey," I say, and she opens her eyes, gazes down at me. Her eyes are glazed with pleasure, and I'm glad to see that. She's trembling, but it isn't with fear.

"Don't stop, Matt. Please don't stop."

"I'm not going to. But we need to move to the backseat, baby. I need room for all the things I want to do to you."

CHAPTER
EIGHTEEN

Evie

I'M OUT OF my depth, floating on a sea of sensation and desire, not knowing what's coming next but wanting it so much. No one ever put his mouth on my breasts before. I had no idea it could feel so thrilling, so amazing. It's as if there's a direct line between my nipples and the little button of pleasure between my legs. Every lick of Matt's tongue makes that button tingle and tighten—and makes me ache so much I don't think anything can ever soothe me.

I climb into the backseat as Matt told me to do, and then he's there, hovering over me, lifting his shirt over his head and dropping it. He goes for the buckle of my belt, loosening it. Then he unzips my jeans and drags them down my hips.

The leather is cool on my naked butt, but it doesn't soothe the flame inside me. Matt takes off my sandals and pulls my jeans the rest of the way off.

It hits me that I'm totally naked now, lying beneath him and ready to fly apart with the lightest of touches. Of course I know what an orgasm is. I've had plenty of them on my own. I've touched myself at night, usually thinking about Matt, and then I come in the quiet stillness of my own bed.

I'm always slightly ashamed and slightly lonely afterward. Ashamed because I feel this compulsion to do it and lonely because it's just me in the end. There's nothing shameful about feeling good, and I know it. But I guess I want more. I want to have orgasms *with* someone.

With Matt.

He kneels above me now, looking down at my body so intensely that I have an urge to cover myself. What if he finds me lacking? What if my body is not as nice as Jeanine's? Is he regretting this and trying to decide how to tell me we need to stop?

My heart hammers in my throat and I start to sit up, but Matt bends over me and captures my lips, his tongue sliding into my mouth, and I sigh. He isn't stopping.

When he breaks the kiss and moves down my throat, I pant with anticipation. His mouth fastens over one of my nipples again, and his hand slides down my belly, down into the curls of my sex. When he skims his fingers into my wetness, I'm simultaneously embarrassed and so turned on I think I might scream.

I want everything and I want it *now*. I'm scared and not scared. I know it's supposed to hurt the first time, but I know that isn't supposed to last very long. I understand what happens during sex. It's not a giant mystery, other than how it *feels*. That I can only imagine.

But if it feels like this feels right now, I think it's going to be pretty amazing.

Matt takes his time on my nipples, sucking and licking and driving me insane. When his mouth glides down my body, his tongue caressing the planes of my belly, I shudder with sharp anticipation.

Will he? *Will he really?*

The thought excites me so much it hurts—and yes, it embarrasses me too. What if he doesn't like it? What if it's awful? What if I smell or taste bad?

"Wait, Matt—" I gasp as his tongue rolls along the line where my pubic hair starts.

He looks up at me, his eyes intense and hot. "Are you scared, Evie?"

"Yes... I mean, I want you to do that, but what if...?"

He laughs softly and opens me with his fingers. "Baby, trust me, I'll like it."

"I've never... I mean, I know you can do this and still be a virgin, but I've never... No one has ever..."

God, I can't even talk. I'm hot, and more than half of it's mortification heating my blood.

"Oh hell, you have no idea how much that turns me on."

And then he lowers his head and his tongue touches me right in the center of all that heat. I moan. I can't help it.

"Evie, damn, you are so sweet," he murmurs, the vibration of his voice against me making the sensation even more intense.

I don't think I breathe through much of it. Well, of course I breathe, but I feel like all I'm doing is moaning and whimpering. Matt licks every sensitive spot I have. He presses the flat of his tongue against me and then flicks my clitoris again and again.

The pressure inside me is incredible. I'm so wet I feel the moisture trickle onto my thighs. Or maybe that's him. I don't know, but I do know that my orgasm rolls over me like a tsunami that I never see coming. I mean, yes, I expect an orgasm, especially since I've never had a guy eat me out before, but this… Whoa, *this*.

It makes sweat break out on my skin. It makes my back arch and my legs shake. It makes me scream and gasp and sob.

Never—*never* have I felt anything like this before.

When I stop shaking, when I finally open my eyes and meet the gaze of the boy I love so much, he's grinning down at me.

"Good?"

All I can do is nod. Matt unbuttons his jeans and takes them off. His erection springs up, big and hard and foreign. Yes, I know what a penis looks like. I've never touched one though.

I reach for him, surprised at how hot and smooth he is. He grips my hand and wraps it around him, and I'm surprised again at the feel of a hard penis. It's kinda, I don't know, rubbery in a way. Not soft or flimsy, but smooth and living and flexible in the sense that it springs back when you squeeze it.

"That's amazing," I say.

He makes a choked sound as I tighten my grip again.

"Yeah," he says tightly. "Amazing."

He reaches for something, and then he's tearing open a foil packet, pulling out a condom. I let him go while he rolls it on. He settles between my thighs, holding himself up with one hand on the seat back and one pressing down beside my head.

"It'll hurt a little," he says.

"I know."

"I'll go slow, but I can't make it not hurt at all."

I settle my hands on his sides. "I know. It's okay."

He lowers his head and kisses me. I taste myself on him. It's odd in a way and so incredibly special too. It isn't bad… just different.

He kisses me deeply—and then I feel him, the head of his penis at my entrance. My heart beats a crazy rhythm and my body shakes. This is it. Really and truly it. The moment when Matt and I are joined together. The moment he'll know the truth about us.

His entry isn't as easy as I hoped. Yes, I'm very wet, but there's still a barrier that he reaches almost immediately. His fingers slide up my side, gently pinch a nipple. The sensation is pleasurable, exciting.

And yet I'm so focused on his body entering mine that I can't relax as much as I should. I want this so much, and I don't want to fail.

"It's okay, Evie," he says against my lips. "It's going to be so good when I'm inside you. Just relax."

He stops tweaking my nipple and moves to my clitoris. When he touches me there, it's like he set off an explosion inside me. I don't come, but I feel his touch in every nerve ending, every cell. My legs go weak—

And he pushes deeper into me. There's a sting of pain as he moves forward, and then the sting stops and he slides completely inside me.

"Wow," he whispers. "Oh fucking wow."

CHAPTER
NINETEEN

Matt

NO, THIS IS not my first time. Not even close to my first time. But holy shit, it feels fucking amazing. I've been with a virgin before—when I was still a virgin too—and it didn't feel like this at all. That was exciting and amazing in its own way, but it wasn't like this.

I feel like I'm on top of the world right now. I feel safe for some inexplicable reason.

I also feel like I'm doing something wrong. Like I've taken Evie's virginity but I've somehow tricked her into it. That I should have been firmer with her and refused.

I know how she feels about me. I know she has a crush on me, and I know that the first time for a girl is emotional. There's more she wants, and I know that too.

But here I am, taking her innocence without any intentions of making promises to her for a future. I care about Evie more than I care about anyone but my sister. I've made a mess of our relationship by doing this, but right now, I don't fucking care. All I care about is the ex-quisite pleasure I feel right this moment.

"You okay?" I ask.

"Yes. It stung, but yes, it's okay now."

Funny how the words *it's okay* are acceptable in this situation but wouldn't be if she was more experienced.

I glide my hand down her side, around the curve of her ass, and lift her leg to curl it around me.

"You ready for what comes next?"

"More than you know."

I start to move inside her, slowly at first because I don't know if she's still hurting no matter what she said to me. But she lifts her hips to meet me, and I know she's feeling it. Feeling this same crazy tightening in her body that I feel in mine.

My balls are tight and lightning streaks through me as I move. I won't last long. I can't. It's too good, and I'm too far gone to pull back from the edge.

I don't think she'll come like this, not the first time, so I put my hand between us.

"Matt!" she cries as I find her sweet spot and work it.

"Baby, this is so good," I tell her, sweat beading on my forehead and running down the sides of my face. I keep pumping into her, not stopping, not letting up.

She keeps thrusting against me, so I know she's good. I'm going to make her come and then come after her, but she reaches her peak so quickly, her body shaking as she moans, that I have to kiss her and feel those cries in my mouth.

Her tongue is crazy against mine, her moans and cries vibrating in my throat as she rocks into me.

I come much too soon, my body stiffening as I keep thrusting my hips into her, my cock exploding inside her, pumping out so much cum I'm worried about the condom breaking.

I pull out of her quicker than I want to, saying a silent prayer of thanks when the condom is intact.

"Oh my God," she says a few seconds later. "That was amazing."

She's lying there with her legs spread and a fine sheen of sweat on her body. Her chest heaves as she sucks in air.

I left the Escalade running and the air on, but it isn't quite enough in the close confines of the vehicle. I sit up and lean back against the seat, removing the condom and twisting a knot into it.

Evie drags herself up until she's leaning against the door. She's so pretty sitting there. So pretty that I want to do it again.

I have every intention of doing it again. I mean I shouldn't have done it in the first place, but now that I have, I'm totally getting inside her again.

Maybe I'll take her out a couple of times in the next week. Maybe I'll take her out every night before I leave. I can take her home when the old man isn't there, fuck her in my bed. God, that would be sweet.

I tug her into my arms, in spite of the warmth, slide my hands over her slick skin. She wraps her arms around me. I push the damp strands of her long hair back over her shoulder and kiss her. It's a soft kiss, but my dick hardens anyway.

"I knew it would be perfect," she says when we stop kissing. "I knew everything would make sense after this."

I smile at her. "What makes sense, *cher*?"

She lowers her gaze from mine, her lashes fanning over her flushed cheeks. "You and me."

"I'm not sure any of it makes sense to me, but okay."

Her eyes are far less certain when they meet mine this time. Almost wounded. Definitely surprised. "How can you say that?"

I shrug, sensing I'm on shaky ground here. "I just mean that you've been my best friend for so many years that crossing into this kind of territory is a little confusing. I don't want to ruin our friendship."

"How would it ruin our friendship?" She seems genuinely puzzled.

I'm starting to feel vaguely uncomfortable, but I'm not sure why. Then again, I know, don't I? I cannot be so fucking stupid as to think she isn't affected by what we just did.

And now I have to be so careful with her, have to make sure she understands. And I have to do it without breaking her heart. Yeah, right.

But I have to. This isn't happily ever after or any of that bullshit.

"Evie, baby, you do realize what this is, right? It's sex. We had sex. Nothing has changed besides that. We were friends—we're still friends. And now we're friends with benefits."

Her eyes widen as she sits back. "Friends with benefits? Seriously? Is that what you think this is?"

That bad feeling inside me swirls higher now, the dark clouds of it threatening to exterminate the light of everything that is beautiful about this.

"What else can it be? I'm leaving next week. You're staying here. This isn't true love or romance or shit. We fucked. We can fuck again. You're still my best friend and that's not going to change."

Oh man, I know when I say it how wrong I am. It *is* changing. It *has* changed. I changed it the minute I stuck my tongue in her mouth back at the cabin. I made the choice, and now I'm dealing with the fallout.

She frowns hard, but then she reaches for her clothes and starts sorting them out. I watch her yank on her panties and jerk on her bra, my stomach sinking into the ground with every angry motion she makes.

I've pissed her off and I don't know how to fix it. But I can't lie to her. I can't tell her I'm going to be the man of her dreams. I can't promise I'll come back for her and whisk her away with me.

"Take me back to the party, Matt."

"I'll take you home."

"NO." Her eyes flash as I stare at her. "You are *not* deciding where I go right now, you got that? I went to the party with Julie and Jack and I'm leaving with them. Now take me back there and stop acting like you give a shit, Matt. Because you *don't*."

I grab my clothes and start to jerk them on. My chest is tight with anger. I get my jeans on, and then I stop and point at her, my finger right in her face.

"You fucking asked for this, Evie. It was *your* idea. I didn't promise you a goddamn thing—and you didn't say you wanted anything either. You asked me to be your first. I was. If you're changing the terms now, that's your own goddamned fault."

Her lip quivers and it just about kills me. But I don't move, don't take her in my arms or apologize the way I suddenly want to do.

"No, you're right. You did exactly as I asked. Now please keep doing what I ask and take me back to the party."

CHAPTER
TWENTY

Evie

I'M ANGRY AND hurt and cursing myself at the same time. Oh, he's right that I didn't say I wanted anything else. I was so sure that everything would be perfect after we made love for the first time. So damn sure.

What an idiot I am. I'm in love with Matt Girard. Have been for years. And even though he is my first lover, even though we were just as close as it's possible for two people to be, his view of me hasn't changed.

Or hasn't changed *much*. I'm not a little sister to be protected anymore. I'm a friend with benefits. A fuck buddy. Someone you can have sex with when there isn't anyone else available.

Oh, it hurts. It hurts so much.

I get into the front seat and cross my arms, staring out the window at the darkness. My eyes are blurry. Matt gets out of the Escalade. Just as I start to wonder what he's doing, he gets inside again and puts it into gear. I told him to take me back to the party, but I don't know if he's going to listen to me or not.

If he takes me home, I'll scream. I'm too raw to process this by myself in my room just yet. I want the party. I want people and laughter—and alcohol. I need to dull this pain. I need distraction.

How can I have been so wrong? How can I believe we are meant to be when he consistently proves we aren't? What if he's right and I'm wrong?

I'm surprised when he drives back to the party instead of to my house. I half expected him to ditch me at home in some sort of misguided effort to protect me. Too late for that.

When we reach the party, I'm out of the Escalade before he's even stopped fully.

"Evie!" He shouts at me but I keep going. I run up the steps and inside. The party's in full swing, and people are even drunker than they were when I left.

I go over to the fridge and pull out a wine cooler. I need this damn thing so much.

"Oh my God."

I jump at the sound of the voice, whirling to find Julie standing there looking up at me.

"What?" I ask, an edge to my voice that says I might burst into tears at any minute.

Julie moves closer, pitching her voice low. "Honey, you look like you've been, well, what you've probably been doing. You need to go in the bathroom and fix your hair and makeup before too many people notice."

I look at the room. Most people are preoccupied with what they're doing, but a few of the girls are looking at me. Some smirk knowingly.

I head for the bathroom, Julie on my heels.

"Well, was it any good? What happened? Did he really…?"

I reach the bathroom, which is thankfully unoccupied, and stand just inside it with a hand on the door when I turn back to Julie.

"Yes, it was good. Yes, he really did. But Jules…" Here I have to suck down the tears welling inside. "Let's just say nothing has changed."

"Oh Evie, I'm so sorry. He's an asshole if he doesn't cherish you."

"Well, he doesn't, so I guess he is definitely an asshole."

An asshole I still love, in spite of how hurt I am. This little voice in my head keeps telling me it's my fault. I should have tried harder, or done more. I should have made my feelings clear. I rushed it when I should have waited, maybe until he came home on vacation from college.

So many damn things I should have, could have, would have done—and I don't know if any of them would have changed the outcome. I've been spectacularly deluded about what was going to happen when I gave myself to Matt.

I close the bathroom door and stand inside with my back to it, breathing deeply. My reflection definitely says I've been rolling around in a bed or somewhere. My makeup is smeared beneath my eyes and my hair is messy. And, crap, I left my purse in Matt's car.

There's a knock on the door a few seconds later and I suck in a breath. "Occupied," I call out.

"It's me," Julie says. "I have your purse."

I open the door and take it gratefully, not even caring how she got it from Matt. Then I set about fixing my hair and makeup as best I can. Difficult when my eyes are so red with the tears I keep swiping away, but I persevere. I drink the entire wine cooler and I pee, wincing at the tenderness between my legs.

Great, now I have a reminder of what I did with Matt. Who knows how long it will last, though I feel like I'll be sore for a while…

When I finally feel I can reappear, I march out of the bathroom with my head held high. Yeah, I just lost my virginity. Yeah, it was pretty amazing.

Julie is sitting with some of the other girls, and they're laughing about something. I join them. I deliberately do not look at Matt. I feel him looking at me from across the room, but I am not going to make eye contact.

Julie nudges me. "I don't know what happened, but he's over there slamming back the whiskey like he's pissed off about something."

I don't care. Let him get drunk. Let him make an ass of himself. It's not my problem. I just pray he won't attempt to drive home.

Missy Sue leans forward into the circle of girls, her eyes glowing as they land on me. "So how was it, Evie? Is he as good as all the girls say he is?" She cuts her gaze to Matt for a second. "Dude, what I wouldn't give to have Matt Girard naked somewhere."

I blink at her. Well, hell, what had I expected anyway? It had to be kind of obvious. I left with Matt over an hour ago, and then I returned with messy hair and smeared makeup. I swig back some of the wine cooler.

"He definitely is," I say, realizing all the girls are watching me expectantly. Eagerly. Apparently, getting down and dirty with Matt Girard is to be envied.

Missy Sue's eyes gleam. "Details, Evie. Details."

I force a laugh. My heart is still too raw for that. "Now that's something you'll have to find out for yourself," I say. "Go ask him. I'm sure he'll whisk you off in his car somewhere."

Missy Sue looks disappointed as she cuts her eyes over to where he's standing. "I can't do that. I'd be too afraid he'd tell me no."

"Nah," I drawl, taking a drink. "He's easy. He'll screw anything that moves."

And that, I realize with a sinking heart, is utterly the truth. He took my virginity because I offered it. Not because he cared. Not because he wanted more from me than my friendship. I offered sex and he accepted. It wasn't special or monumental for him. It meant nothing at all.

One week from now, he's leaving town. But I've already lost him. I just didn't realize it until it was too late.

CHAPTER TWENTY-ONE

Matt

I LOOK AT my room one last time. My suitcases are packed and this is it. I'm finally getting the fuck out of here. For good. And yet my heart aches too. It wasn't all bad, was it? My mama was a wonderful woman and we had a real home when she was alive. There were times when I loved living here, where the bayou calls to me and the land is in my ancestors' blood and therefore in mine. This house is so much more than four walls that only contain sorrow and pain.

It had once—many times, I am sure—contained laughter and love as well.

And it probably will again someday.

I close the door and go downstairs. My sister is there, and Mrs. Simpson. My father is not. Evie is not. My heart pinches tight as I think of her.

What a fucking mess I made of that situation. I ruined our friendship, a friendship that existed for years and went through a lot. She was there for me when my mama died. She comforted me and distracted me from my father's rages as I got older, though I never let her know what my father was really like. I didn't want anyone to know.

Even when we grew apart, I knew Evie was there if I needed her.

But I ruined it all. I took her virginity in the backseat of my daddy's Cadillac, and then I got drunk and stupid and spilled the details to people I shouldn't have.

It's been one week since the party, one week since that night, and I haven't spoken to Evie again. I thought about calling her. I wanted to call her. But I don't know what to say, so I finally erased her number from my phone and told myself to get over it and move on.

She was over it. She ran from me when I took her back to the party and she didn't look at me the rest of the evening. I carried her purse inside because she forgot it in the car, but her cousin took it from me and I never got to talk to her.

Evie hasn't called me or spoken to me since that night. So it isn't just me, right? It's her too. She's letting me know she's finished with me.

It left me empty inside, but I deserve it. I'm used to feeling empty. Used to fucking things up. Candy hadn't loved me though she pretended she did. Evie thought she loved me but she really didn't. I'm not lovable. I'm fucked up and self-centered. I don't deserve to be loved, not like that.

Christina loves me, but that's different. Mrs. Simpson loves me. Bonnie does too. They've been here since I was a baby and they forgave me for my excesses. I can see it in their kind eyes and warm smiles. I may not deserve it, but

I have it anyway.

I say my good-byes, complete with hugs and tears from the women, and then I get into my car and drive down the long drive for the last time. Well, the last time for a very long time. I'm not coming back on breaks. There's nothing to come back for. Maybe one day I will. But I don't know when.

I drive through town, my gut churning as I pass the beauty shop. I'm not planning to do it, but I find myself turning onto the street that will take me toward Evie's house. I drive through the historic section of town where the lawns are wide, the trees are shady, and the houses are old and stately.

I pass over the railroad tracks and into the shabbier side of town. These houses are old too, smaller, the lawns not as wide or stately. There's a movement to put this section into the historic district, but it hasn't gained enough support yet.

I hesitate at Evie's street. My car is distinctive, noticeable. I'm planning to sell it since I can't have a car at West Point, but for now it's the only car I have. I sit at the end of the street for long minutes, until a car pulls up behind me and honks.

My heart kicks higher. I want to turn onto Evie's street, roll past her house one last time. Maybe she'll see me and come outside. Maybe we can have one last talk, one last good-bye.

But I'm a coward. The car behind me honks again, and I mash the gas, going straight rather than turning.

I'm angry with myself, and then I'm not. As I drive toward the city limits, I feel like a weight is lifted. This is it. The end of my life in Rochambeau and the start of it somewhere else. I can't take all this baggage with me. I can't keep trying to push the boulder up the hill and hope it doesn't crush me on the way back down.

I drag in a breath and then another, feeling lighter the farther I get from town.

Evie will be all right. Hell, she'll be better than all right. Without me in the picture, she'll move on and get over her crush. She'll have a good life. She'll find a great guy, get married, have kids someday.

Maybe what happened between us is for the best. She's seen me for what I am, and she's moved on. It's time I moved on too.

I step on the gas and drive faster, flying toward Baton Rouge and the highway that will take me into another life…

~

The story of Matt and Evie doesn't end here.
If you want to find out what happens when they meet
again, the story continues in
Hot Pursuit,
Book 1 of the Hostile Operations Team Series.
Keep reading for a sample.

HOT PURSUIT

LYNN RAYE

NEW YORK TIMES & USA TODAY BESTSELLING AUTHOR

HARRIS

PROLOGUE

Two months ago…

SOMETHING WAS WRONG.

It wasn't anything obvious, but Captain Matthew Girard felt it in his gut nonetheless. It was an itching sensation across his skin, a buzzing in his belly. Perhaps it was simply the weight of this mission pressing down on him. Though the Hostile Operations Team always performed critical missions, this one was even more so. Failure was not an option.

Beside him, Kevin MacDonald lay in the sand, his camouflage-clad form as still as marble until the moment he turned his head and caught Matt's eye.

Kev's hand moved. Doesn't feel right, he signaled.

No, Matt signaled back. Count on Kev to pick up on it too. They'd been on a shitload of ops together. Matt knew that if his second-in-command was picking up on this weird vibe, it wasn't just him. Yet the mission was too important to scrub without more than just a gut feeling to go on.

"It's awful quiet in that compound." Jim Matuzaki's voice came through the earpiece a few moments later.

"Yeah," Matt answered into the mic attached to his helmet. Almost as if the tangos inside knew that a HOT squad was coming and had abandoned the compound.

The stone structure thirty meters away rose two stories high and lacked windows. The roof was flat to enable gunmen to look out on the surrounding territory and defend the building.

But there were no gunmen. Not tonight.

In the surveillance photos, the gunmen were so plentiful they'd stood out against the pale roof like a porcupine's quills. And now…

Nothing.

Though it was quiet here, gunfire exploded in the distance at regular intervals. A pitched battle between a pocket of enemy forces and a Ranger battalion raged a few miles away. HOT's mission was quieter, but no less deadly.

They were here for Jassar ibn-Rashad, heir to Freedom Force leader Al Ahmad. But this mission was different. Usually, they killed the target. Tonight, they were extracting him. The rumored new Freedom Force mastermind was wanted higher up in the chain, and Matt didn't question orders from the Pentagon. They wanted him, they were getting him.

Matt and his team had planned the mission to kidnap ibn-Rashad for weeks. Down to the last damn detail. And then they'd gotten word just a few days ago that ibn-Rashad was moving to this location.

The intel was good. Damn good. And their contact had been reliable on more than one occasion.

But this time?

The bad feeling in Matt's gut was getting stronger by the second. He'd thought the kid seemed more nervous than usual the last time he'd gone to meet with him. The kid had always been nervous, but he'd seemed to trust Matt's word. And Matt had trusted him as much as he was able. Trust, but verify.

Which the CIA had done. All the chatter indicated that ibn-Rashad had moved to this location. Nothing indicated that the Freedom Force had any idea they were being targeted. And in spite of the niggling feeling he'd had about the whole thing, Matt had chosen to press forward with the op.

Just then, a light flashed up on the roof and blinked out again. Male voices carried in the night, followed by a bark of laughter.

"Two men," Marco San Ramos said over the headset. "Smoking."

Marco and Jim were closer and had a better view through the glasses.

"Richie?" Jim's voice came through the headset again, calling Matt by his team name.

He knew what the other man was asking. What they were all waiting for. In another location close by, Billy Blake, Jack Hunter, Chase Daniels, and Ryan Gordon also waited for the signal to go or to retreat. The timeline was tight, and if they didn't go in now, they'd have to scrub the mission. They had precisely twenty minutes to infiltrate the compound, kill the tangos, and extract ibn-Rashad.

If they were going in.

"Mission is a go." Matt made the split-second decision in spite of the acid roiling in his belly. What if they didn't get a second chance at this? Lives hung in the balance with ibn-Rashad remaining free. This mission had always been risky, but what did they ever do that wasn't?

Failing was simply not a part of his genetic makeup. Maybe he got it from the old man—that combination of stubbornness, meanness, and sheer cockiness that wouldn't let him back down unless there was no other option. He wasn't stupid, but he wasn't a quitter either. And people's lives hung in the balance.

People he could save. He'd made a promise, long ago, and he'd kept it. He was still keeping it.

"Repeat," Matt said, his jaw tight, "mission is a go."

"Copy," Jim replied. The rest of the men chimed in. Seconds later, two cracks rang in the night. And then Billy's voice came over the headset. "Targets on roof neutralized."

Matt let out a breath he hadn't realized he'd been holding. Jack "Hawk" Hunter could always be counted on to make the difficult shots. The dude was probably the best sharpshooter Matt had ever seen. Thank God.

Everything went like clockwork from that point on. They converged on the compound from their separate locations. Kev set a charge on the door and then it exploded inward. Billy tossed a flash-bang into the opening. It went off with a loud crack, the light flaring for a split second as bright as a nuclear flash. Whoever was in that room would be temporarily blind and disoriented after that baby went off.

The team rushed through the door, going right and left in succession, guns drawn, as pandemonium reigned inside. HOT worked like a well-oiled machine. Each man knew instinctively where to shoot, could have done so blindfolded.

Within seconds, the terrorists lay dead and the scent of spent gunpowder hung heavy in the air, along with the odors of smoke and stale sweat.

Sweat also trickled down the inside of Matt's assault suit. He didn't have time to be uncomfortable. Instead, he and Kev raced up the steps along with Marco and Jim, searching for ibn-Rashad, while the other guys secured the perimeter.

A methodical sweep of the rooms proved futile.

"He's not here," Marco spat. "There's no one else."

"Goddamn." The skin-crawling sensation Matt had had from the beginning of this op was now a full-blown assault on his senses. Kev looked at him, his face bleak behind the greasepaint, his eyes saying everything Matt was thinking.

Jassar ibn-Rashad was supposed to be here. He'd been reported here as of this afternoon, in fact. There was a price on the man's head and no reason to move from this location... unless he'd been tipped off they were coming.

Sonofabitch. Matt suddenly felt like he was standing in a lightning storm, holding a steel rod in the air. He wasn't necessarily going to be struck down, but the possibility was damn good.

"Do another sweep for intel. West side. Three minutes, and we're out," Matt ordered.

"Copy," Marco said. He and Jim headed for the west side of the house while Matt and Kev split up to cover the rooms at the east end. Matt swept into each room, weapon drawn, helmet light blazing. There was nothing. No papers, no computers, no media of any kind. Nothing they could use to determine what ibn-Rashad was planning next.

He hit the hall again and met up with Kev, who shook his head.

Jim and Marco arrived next, empty-handed. The four of them pounded down the stairs. Another quick sweep of the rooms on the ground floor, and they were back into the night with the rest of the team, running for the extraction point five miles away.

They hadn't gone a mile when bullets blasted into the air beside them. A hot, stinging sensation bloomed in Matt's side. He kept running anyway. Until they crested the dune they'd been traveling up and came face-to-face with a series of rocket-propelled grenade launchers pointed right at them.

ONE

Rochambeau, Louisiana
Present day

"MM-MM, LOOK AT that Girard boy, all grown up and better looking than a man ought to be," said one of the ladies under the row of hairdryers.

Evie Baker's heart did a somersault. *Matt Girard. Dear God.* "Careful," Stella Dupre yelped as warm water sprayed against the side of the sink and hit her in the face.

"Sorry." Evie shifted the hose.

She was a chef, not a shampoo girl, but she didn't suppose that distinction mattered anymore since the bank now owned her restaurant. Shampoo girl in her mama's beauty salon was just about the only job she could get at the moment, in spite of the resumes she'd blasted to every culinary school contact she could think of. The economy was bad and no one was hiring—and she didn't have the luxury of waiting for something else to come along.

She didn't think her skills would rust anytime soon, but it hurt not to be cooking right now. She should be playing with recipes, tweaking the flavors, and experimenting with new combinations. Instead, she was rinsing hair for a host of Stella Dupres—and doing it badly, apparently.

Mama glanced over at her, frowning even as the snip-snip of scissors continued unabated. The ladies in the salon swung to look out the picture window as Matt strode along, and the chatter ratcheted up a notch. The odor of perming solution and floral shampoo surrounded Evie like a wet blanket, squeezing her lungs. Her breath stuttered in her chest.

Matt Girard. She hadn't seen him in ten years. Not since that night when he'd taken her virginity and broken her heart all at once. She'd known he was back in town—hell, the whole town had talked of nothing else since his arrival yesterday. She'd even known this moment was inevitable, except that she'd been doing her best to avoid all the places he might be for as long as possible.

They'd had an easy relationship, once. The kind where he could tug her ponytail, drop a frog in her shirt, or tease her endlessly about her buckteeth—which, thank God, she no longer had. But that had been when they were kids. Then she'd gotten breasts and started blushing whenever he looked her way, and things had changed. Or at least they had for her.

Matt, however, had been determined not to see her as anything other than little Evie Baker, the tomboy he used to play with when her mama went out to Reynier's Retreat every week to fix his sick mother's hair. He'd apparently persisted in that belief until the night she'd asked him, after a single shot of whiskey to give her courage, to be her first.

She'd had so many stupid dreams, and he'd crushed

them all. But not before he gave her what she'd asked him for.

"Heard he got shot out there in Iraq," Mrs. Martin said as Evie's mama rolled a lock of gray hair around a fat pink curler.

"Yes indeed, got a Purple Heart," Mama said. "The senator was right proud, according to Lucy Greene."

"That's not what I heard!" Joely Hinch crowed. "Miss Mildred told me he's being kicked out of the Army because he didn't obey orders."

"Fiddlesticks," Mrs. Martin said. "That boy bleeds red, white, and blue. Same as his daddy and every last Girard that ever was born up in that big house."

Joely crossed her arms, looking slightly irritated to be contradicted. "You just wait and see," she said smugly.

"Shush up, y'all," Mama said. "I think he's coming in."

Evie's heart sank to her toes. She wasn't ready for this. Not on top of everything else. She was feeling so bruised and battered after her failure with the restaurant. She did not need Matt Girard swaggering back into her life and making her feel all the chaotic emotions she'd once felt for him.

She finished Stella's shampoo and wrapped her hair in a towel. "I'm not tipping you, Evangeline." Stella sniffed. "You have to be more careful than that."

"I know. And I don't blame you at all." Except, of course, she desperately needed every penny she could get if she hoped to escape this town again. It wasn't that Rochambeau was bad—it's that it was bad for *her*. Always had been.

Here, she always felt like the awkward kid who lived

in a tiny cottage with her mama and wore secondhand clothes because that's all they could afford. Didn't matter that the clothes were no longer secondhand, or that she wasn't a kid anymore. Or that she didn't care if the girls who lived in the nice big houses with the manicured lawns didn't like her; she still felt like that girl who wanted so desperately to fit in.

And the biggest part of fitting in had, at one time, relied on the man striding toward her mama's salon like he didn't have a care in the world. Evie's heart did a somersault as he reached the door.

Magazines snapped open in a flurry as the ladies tried to appear casually disinterested in the six-foot-two hunk of muscle about to open the glass door. More than one pair of eyes peeked over the tops of glossy pages as he stepped up to the sidewalk from the street.

No way in hell was she sticking around for this. It wouldn't take these ladies more than a few moments to remember the scandalous rumors about her and Matt, and she didn't want to be here when they did.

"If you'll excuse me, I have to get some things out of the back." Without waiting for a reply, she strode toward the stockroom. Rachel Mayhew, Mama's regular shampoo girl, looked up and smiled as she passed. Rachel was only twenty, so she probably didn't know about Evie's disastrous night with Matt. Or maybe she did, considering the way this town talked.

What should have been Evie's own private shame had all too quickly become common knowledge back then. Part of that was her own fault, and part was Matt's—but she still wasn't sticking around to endure the sidelong glances and whispered conversations.

Life had beaten her up enough recently and she wasn't in the mood to feel like a wounded teenager today.

A month ago, she'd said goodbye to her dream. It still hurt. Her lovely little bistro in Florida was now in the bank's hands, and all because she'd trusted a man. Or mostly because she'd trusted a man.

Her restaurant, Evangeline's, hadn't exactly been doing a booming business, but things had been getting better and growth had been steady. It had, for a time, flourished under David's management, which was how she'd grown to trust his insistence that he knew what he was doing and that she should spend her time perfecting her recipes instead of worrying over the mundane details.

David was cocky, charming, and utterly confident. She'd found that intriguing. One thing had led to another, and they'd ended up sharing a bed from time to time. She'd liked David, thought they were on the same page. He was an accountant who loved to cook, who knew a lot about social media and advertising, and who increased her profits by a few simple—or so he'd said—marketing tricks.

All of it lies. He'd increased her profits, yes. But then he'd robbed her blind. She'd seen the books on a regular basis and never known anything was out of whack. He hadn't meant her to know, of course, but it still bugged her that she hadn't seen through David's schemes.

No, she'd been so thrilled with the way things were going that she'd spent more time doing what she really loved—cooking and creating recipes for the Cajun fusion dishes she'd become known for in their community. A mistake that she still kicked herself over, even though David had covered his tracks too well for her to see anything amiss.

She'd trusted him. But how had she not known he was bad news? How had she let herself be fooled by a handsome face and charming manners?

She'd learned in the aftermath of the destruction he'd wrought that the authorities thought he had ties to organized crime. He'd been skimming money, along with other more nefarious schemes such as money laundering and extortion. She hated to think about it. Evangeline's had been everything she'd ever wanted when she'd broken out of her hometown and gone to cooking school a few years ago.

But here she was again, back in Rochambeau and washing hair in her mama's salon, just like when she'd been in high school. *Loser.* All she wanted was to get out again at the first opportunity. Before that loser feeling wrapped around her throat and squeezed the rest of her dreams away.

Matt reached for the door, and Evie darted behind the stockroom curtain. Her heart slammed against her ribs as the tinkling bell announced his arrival. She turned to lean against the doorjamb and pushed the rose-print polyester aside with one finger. She was being silly. He wasn't here because of her. He was here because his sister had sent him on some errand or other for her wedding.

Hell, he probably wouldn't even blink twice if he ran smack into her.

Evie frowned. Her eyes slid down his body and back up again. He was still something to look at. Something easy on the eyes and hard on the senses.

He'd changed in ten years, but some things were still the same. That cocky swagger as he'd approached the shop. He'd always walked like his daddy owned all the oil in the Gulf of Mexico. Which he damn near did. The Girards had been Rochambeau's wealthiest family for as long as anyone could remember.

Matt's dark hair was cut very short, and his shoulders were much broader than when he'd been seventeen. The fabric of his white cotton T-shirt stretched across a wide chest packed with muscle. His bare forearms made her throat go dry.

Something quivered deep inside her, the way it always had from the moment she'd become aware of Matt as more than a boy she played with. Something hot and dark and secret. Evie squashed the feeling ruthlessly.

He pushed a hand through his hair, every muscle of his torso seeming to bunch and flex with the movement. She would have sworn she heard a collective sigh from the ladies in the salon. Rachel absently ran water in her sink, cleaning out the soap bubbles from the last shampoo. When she got too close to the edge, the water sprayed up into her face.

Evie would have laughed if she too weren't caught up in Matt's every move. She'd adored him ten years ago and worshipped him until the night she'd given him her virginity.

What a mistake that had been. Not because the sex had been awful. No, it'd been pretty exciting, all things considered. It was what had happened afterward that ruined it for her. The shift in their relationship hadn't been what she'd expected. And then he'd been such an ass about it.

"Afternoon, ladies." Matt tipped his head to them.

"Afternoon," they murmured in unison, voices sugary

and lilting, eyes assessing and cataloging him.

"Miz Breaux." He took her mother's hand and kissed it like a courtier.

"Oh, shoot." She smacked him playfully on the shoulder. "What do you want? Don't you know this is a beauty parlor? Sid's Barber Shop is on Main Street."

"Well, ma'am." He grinned that devil-may-care grin Evie remembered so well. "I figured Old Sid can't see so well anymore and I'm still fond of my ears. I'd much rather have a lady's touch, if you know what I mean."

"Oh my." Mama giggled. *Giggled.*

Evie rolled her eyes. No wonder she couldn't pick a decent man. She came by the defect genetically. Mama had been divorced three times. She'd gone back to using her maiden name after the second one in order to avoid confusion. Evie had her daddy's last name, her sixteen-year-old sister had a different name, and Mama had yet another one.

"You don't even look like you need a haircut," Mama was saying.

He scrubbed a hand over the nape of his neck. "My sister thinks I do. And it's her wedding."

Mama giggled again. What was it about that man that turned even the smartest woman into an airhead? "Well, we can't let Christina be disappointed then, can we? But you'll have to wait until I finish with Mrs. Martin."

Mama gestured toward the pink vinyl seats in the front of the shop, and Matt gave her the famous Girard smile that used to melt the female hearts of Rochambeau High School. Evie felt a little hitch in her own heart, in spite of herself.

Why did he still have to be so damn good-looking?

Was it too much to ask for him to be balding or growing a potbelly? Apparently so. Mother Nature was cruel.

"Sure thing, Miz Breaux."

Before he'd taken three steps toward the waiting area, Mama said, "You remember my daughter, Evangeline, don't you? She was a year behind you in school. Y'all used to play when I'd come out to do your mama's hair every week."

Evie's heart crashed into her ribs. The ladies in the shop grew quiet while they waited for his answer. She knew what they were thinking. What they were waiting for. Why should it bother her what they thought? What any of them thought?

It had been ten years ago, and it didn't matter anymore. She was grown up. Matt was grown up. Who cared?

Except that's not how Rochambeau worked, and she knew it. It might have been ten years, but he'd humiliated her. He'd broken her heart and tossed her to the wolves when she wasn't prepared to deal with the consequences of her actions. Not that anyone knew for sure what had happened, but rumors were usually enough in Rochambeau.

"Yes, ma'am, I sure do. How is she?" He didn't sound in the least bit remorseful. But why would he? He'd departed for college a week later, and she'd been the one left behind to pick up the pieces.

"Evie's great," Mama announced. "Been living in Florida, but she's home now. Maybe you can talk to her while you wait. Y'all can catch up."

Evie's stomach plummeted to her toes. Oh no. No, no, *no*. What if she went into the bathroom and refused to come out? Or just quietly slipped out the back door and disappeared for a couple of hours? It was time for her lunch break, and—

Coward. Evie stiffened her spine. She wasn't running away. If it wasn't now, it'd be some other time. She couldn't avoid him forever. And far better to get this over with in public, while she could maintain her dignity and show the good people of Rochambeau there was nothing left to talk about.

"That'd be great," he said in an *aw shucks* way she didn't buy for a second. He might talk smooth and act all friendly and *gee-whiz ma'am*, but she knew better. God, did she know better.

He was nothing more than a self-centered, arrogant jerk with a giant sense of entitlement and no mercy for those he considered beneath him. A little corner of her heart still hurt like it had been yesterday, but she ruthlessly stomped on the feeling until it stopped.

"Good," her mother said as if it were the best idea in the world, her gaze sweeping the shop. "She was here just a minute ago. Evie? Evie?"

"She went in the back," Stella offered with what Evie was convinced was a hint of glee. Bitch.

Right. There was nothing Evie could do except face this particular blast from the past. Because there was no way on earth she'd ever let Matt Girard humiliate her again. She'd learned the hard way, but at least she'd learned.

"I'm right here, Mama," she said, whipping off her smock and pushing back the curtain.

TWO

MATT STILL DIDN'T know what he was doing at the Cut 'N Curl, but the second Evie Baker walked out of the stockroom, he felt as if someone had dropped a truckload of cement on his head. He hadn't seen her in ten years, not since the night he'd taken her virginity in the back of his daddy's Cadillac.

He'd never forgotten that night, never forgotten what a dickhead he'd been. He didn't expect she had either, which is why he wasn't surprised that she was currently glaring daggers at him.

Little Evie Baker. Not so little anymore.

He remembered the first time he'd ever seen her, when he'd been seven and his mama had first gotten sick. Norma Breaux always brought Evie with her when she came out to Reynier's Retreat. He hadn't known any of the kids in town because he'd been in private school then, but when Evie didn't scream after he dropped a worm on her, he knew he'd found someone fun to play with. His sister always screamed and hated even a speck of dirt to land on her pretty clothes, but Evie had been as good as any boy when it came to getting dirty.

Matt's temples throbbed. He'd never wanted to hurt her, God knew, but he'd been in a bad place back then. No, he'd been an arrogant, entitled prick. He knew he shouldn't have touched her when she'd asked, but he'd done it anyway.

By that point, he'd been trying for years to ignore the way she'd changed—one day she started wearing dresses and blushing whenever he looked at her; the next she had breasts and curves and he had no clue what to say to her anymore. But then she was there, standing before him with her eyes flashing and her cheeks flushed, and she'd just been so damn pretty, and so damn exciting, that he'd taken her hand, led her out to his daddy's car, and drove them away from the party they'd been at.

He'd felt guilty every moment since, but it was simply another thing to add to the heap of guilt inside his soul. Later, when he'd gotten his head on a bit straighter, he'd thought about calling her to apologize, but too much time had passed. By then he'd figured it was better to let it stay in the past.

A mistake, he thought now. This woman was not happy to see him. There was no pushing aside old mistakes, no going back to a simpler time when they'd gone fishing for crawdads together or sat in a tall tree and watched the gators glide through the bayou.

This Evie Baker was not in a forgiving mood, and he didn't blame her at all.

Still, a very male part of him couldn't help but appreciate her on another level. The level that had gotten him in trouble in the first place.

Evie had been a lovely teenager, but she'd blossomed

into an even lovelier woman. And he shouldn't do a damn thing about it, no matter how much he might want to. If he'd met her in a bar, he'd do everything he could to get her to go home with him.

But she was not a woman in a bar, and he owed her more than that. Matt focused on her pissed-off posture and flashing eyes.

"Evie." She stopped in front of him, arms crossed.

Jesus. She was all curves and sleek skin in a pair of cut-off jean shorts and a body-hugging pink tank top. Her legs were still long, still built to hug a man's waist.

Shit. He didn't need to be thinking that way.

And yet, no matter how hard he tried, he couldn't help it. It was the first thought that sprang to his head when his gaze glided over those legs. He'd kick himself for it later. Right now, he had a bigger problem: keeping his body from responding the way it wanted to at the memory of the last time he'd seen her.

She'd been naked, her lush form arrayed before him, her skin hot, silky, and damp with sweat. She'd been so damn sweet, so innocent. And it'd been a long time since he'd had any sweetness in his life.

"Hi, Matt."

"You're looking all grown up." He could have bit his tongue off when her eyes narrowed.

"It's what happens in ten years." Hostility swirled around her like a tornado.

He stretched his arm along the back of the chair beside him with a casualness he didn't feel. *New tactic*. "So how have you been?"

"Great. You?"

She was smiling now, but he wasn't fooled. Violet

eyes looked back at him with a mixture of embarrassment and fury. He'd done that. He'd put that look on her face, and it bothered him more than he could say.

God, he had a lot to answer for.

"Great," he said, parroting her like an idiot. "Why don't you have a seat?"

She shook her long black ponytail. He remembered wrapping his fists in that hair and tugging when they'd been children. And then he remembered wrapping his hands in her hair for a completely different reason.

"Thanks, but I can't stay. It was nice to see you."

"Wait a minute," he said as she moved away. She stopped and half-turned toward him. He glanced at the ladies watching them. They were just out of earshot, but he leaned forward and pitched his voice lower anyway. "What's your hurry? We've hardly said two words to each other."

He knew the reason, but he didn't want her to go. Not yet. There was something about having her near, something that sparked inside him and made him feel somewhat human again. He didn't know why, and he didn't know if it would last.

But he liked it. For the first time in months, he felt as if he could breathe again. As if he'd come home for real instead of simply going through the motions.

She sighed and turned to face him completely. He got the distinct impression she was calling up some sort of internal armor system in order to deal with him. Definitely not what he was used to in a woman—but then nothing about his relationship with Evie had ever been normal.

Usually, with other women, he was the one with the internal armor. He was the one who pulled away, because he had nothing to offer beyond a few stolen nights before he was back out on a mission.

But dealing with Evie felt completely different.

Her chin thrust out, her eyes flashing cold fire. "It's not personal. I'm just busy. And there's really nothing to say, is there?"

Matt stood. Hesitated when she seemed to shrink away from him. His height and size could be intimidating, he knew, but he hadn't expected that reaction from her of all people. As if she were afraid of him. She'd never been afraid of him, even when he'd jumped out from behind a tree and screamed bloody murder. She'd shrieked, of course—and then she'd socked him.

But this, here and now… it loosened any remaining restraints on his tongue.

"I'm sorry." He hadn't known quite what he would say if he ever saw her again, but that was certainly the least of what he owed her.

"For what?" The question surprised him, though perhaps it shouldn't. Evie Baker never had liked to show any weakness. She glanced over her shoulder to see if anyone was listening, lowered her voice another notch. "I came on to you, remember?"

At least she didn't pretend not to know what he was talking about. He admired that. And he also admired the way she always tried to take responsibility, even when it wasn't her fault. It was frustrating as hell, but so was Evie. She'd never backed down from a challenge in all the time he'd known her.

Still, she wasn't the one at fault here. He was. "Yeah, but you probably didn't expect me to brag about it."

Anger slid through him. He'd been such an arrogant

young fuck back then. Stupid. She'd given him her inno-cence, and he'd trampled it in the dirt like it was his due. He still had no idea what he'd been thinking when it was over and he'd swaggered back to the party.

He was leaving in a week, going off to West Point, and he remembered being so ready to escape. Ready to get the hell out of his father's house and be his own man. He'd been drunk, stupid, and filled with a rage at the world that he couldn't explain.

Evie shrugged. "What guy wouldn't have told his buddies, especially at that age? It was a long time ago."

He stepped closer, lowered his voice as Rachel May-hew turned off the taps to her latest shampoo customer and cocked an ear in their direction.

"Maybe so, but I shouldn't have done it. We were friends and then—"

Her gaze snapped to his. "Were we? Were we ever?"

He felt her words like a barb to his heart. He deserved them. "I thought so. But I fucked up. I'm sorry."

He didn't bother to tell her he'd been falling-down drunk when he'd spilled the details of their evening to his friends. It wasn't an excuse.

She drew in what he assumed was a calming breath. And then she lifted those lashes and speared him with her pretty eyes again. "You did fuck up. Bad. But nobody gave you a hard time about it. They reserved that for me."

Shame rolled over him. "I know the guys made your life hell after I left."

"Not just the guys. Oh, they thought I was an easy mark, that's certain. But the girls weren't particularly nice either. Well, some of them. It hurt. A lot."

Before he could even begin to answer, to find the

right thing to say, she seemed to shake her head as if clearing away the fog of pain and anger. "Ancient history though. Over and done and not your problem." She glanced down at her bare wrist. "Oh, hey, look, it's time to get going. As much as this little reunion has buoyed my spirits, I gotta run."

"Evie—"

The door chimed then and a petite blond woman barreled inside, stopping Evie in her tracks and cutting off any further apologies Matt tried to make.

He recognized her cousin right away, but Julie Breaux didn't even spare him a glance.

"Hey, Evie, can you see if there's room to fit me in? I want to get my highlights done before the party tonight."

"Sure, let me check the schedule." Evie turned away and the woman started to follow, then came up short as if she'd just realized he was there.

If looks could freeze a guy in his tracks, he'd be stuck here into the next millennium. Julie arched an eyebrow, coolly assessing him.

"Heard you got a whole battalion captured out there in Iraq."

Jesus. There was nothing this town didn't blow out of proportion. Though what he usually did for the military was top secret, the Department of Defense propaganda machine had to work overtime once the Freedom Force took to the airwaves with news of their captives. By the time the DoD was done, Matt and his team looked like average G.I. Joes on a rescue mission rather than part of an elite counter-terrorism unit.

Which was precisely as it should be. There was no compromising the identity of HOT. Ever.

"Nope, it was just a platoon," Matt replied with a sarcasm he didn't feel. Jim Matuzaki and Marco San Ramos weren't ever coming home again because of him. Because he hadn't listened to his gut that night.

Not a day went by when he didn't think about them. Two guys he'd shared dusty foxholes and claustrophobic caves with, who'd watched his back more than once. He'd failed them by not scrubbing that mission. He'd wanted to get Jassar ibn-Rashad and save lives, but he'd lost two instead.

Ibn-Rashad was still out there. Still planning to kill.

And Matt might not ever get a chance to do a damn thing about it. His future with HOT was shaky at best after the failure of the last op. His team had been inactive for weeks while other HOT teams came and went. They'd had to sit and watch others go into the field, knowing they'd failed at their task, knowing others were in danger because of them.

Soon, he'd find out his fate. Next week, when he left Rochambeau, he had to attend a hearing on what had gone wrong out there in the desert. He would take responsibility for what had happened to his team, and he might never go on another operation again. His days in HOT very well could be over.

The place where he'd been shot still throbbed. The bullet—a long, ugly mother called a 7.62x39—had pierced the skin, but it had lost momentum going through his assault suit and gotten stuck without passing into his body. He'd been lucky that day, even if he hadn't deserved it. And luckier still when another HOT squad infiltrated the camp and rescued his team before the rest of them could be killed.

Standing here now, in a beauty salon in Rochambeau, was surreal at best. That sense of unreality he'd been living with for the last couple of months grew stronger. What the hell was he going to do if he got assigned to a desk for the rest of his career? It would, in effect, be a demotion, even if they never stripped him of rank.

And it would mean the end of everything that made any sense to him.

"So how's Christina doing?" Julie asked. "I haven't seen her in a couple of weeks now."

"Fine. Nervous, maybe, but fine."

"That's good. She's nice, your sister." *Unlike you* remained unspoken.

"She is indeed."

Julie's gaze dropped over him then. "So you gonna be at the lake tonight?" she asked, switching gears on him so fast he had to shake off a sense of whiplash.

He looked at Evie, didn't miss the look of disbelief that crossed her face as she glanced up from the appointment book. Her cousin had just performed a one-eighty turn at ninety miles an hour, going from hostile to flirtatious in a heartbeat.

"Probably not."

Julie stuck out her lower lip. "Too bad."

Definitely a sexual vibe there. He tried to imagine it. Couldn't. But he could imagine it with Evie. It'd been far too long since he'd had a woman, and though Evie was the wrong woman for a variety of reasons, he couldn't help but think about it.

"Great news, Jules," Evie said. "Mama can fit you in in about an hour."

"Sounds good," Julie said as she went and leaned on

the counter beside Evie.

"Will you be there tonight?" Matt asked Evie as she penciled her cousin's name in the appointment book. He didn't know why he was asking, since he had to attend a formal dinner for Christina and her fiancé tonight. But he wanted to know.

She looked up, her gaze locking with his, and he felt the jolt inside, right at gut level.

"No."

Julie pinched her arm. "Yes, you will. I promised everyone I'd bring you. You've been in town for almost a month and you keep promising to go. It's been so long, and everyone misses you."

Evie looked skeptical and Matt felt a throb of irritation at her cousin. "I really don't think—" Evie began.

"Aw, Evie, come on. It's just one night. Don't be so stuck up."

"We'll talk about it later." Evie was clearly not happy with the idea. She put the pencil down and grabbed Julie's arm. "Let's go get some lunch. Give your sister my congratulations, in case I don't see her before Saturday," she said to Matt.

The two of them headed for the back of the shop, disappearing behind the same flowered curtain she'd emerged from earlier. Matt turned and sank down on the pink vinyl seat again, feeling oddly numb and out of place.

He was home in a pink nightmare of a salon, Evie hated him, and Jim and Marco were dead. The contrast was so stark, so gut-wrenching. Half the time he just wanted to shout at everyone that they had no idea what kind of things happened out there in the world and how dare they go on as if everything was normal, but the rational part of him knew they wouldn't understand. Not only that, but they'd also think he was crazy.

He thought of Evie's dark hair and flashing eyes. For a few minutes, she'd made him feel grounded. Real. Now he felt the way he had for the past two months: as if he were walking around with his guts on the outside.

"You ready, sugar?" Norma Breaux said then, whipping Matt from his dark thoughts. She shook out a hot-pink plastic smock and wrapped it around his neck as he sat down in her chair.

He was ready for anything these days.

And none of it good.

French Quarter, New Orleans

The files were gone. The computer. Everything. He'd been careless. David West melded into the shadows of the building, peering into the dark alley. Rivera's grunts had been in his room. He couldn't go back, nor could he verify what he knew to be true. But he didn't need to. He'd seen them, seen Brianna Sweeney leaving with her two thugs in tow.

Once, he'd been one of them, doing as he was told, moving into an area and enforcing Ryan Rivera's will. He'd been the bean counter, much higher on the brain meter than any of those three, but he knew them intimately. Had worked with them countless times.

Most recently with Brianna in Florida at a place called Evangeline's. He thought he'd evaded the organization this time, but sonofabitch if he hadn't quite done it after all.

He'd wanted out, but apparently once Rivera had a hold of you, you never got out.

Cold sweat dripped down his spine. He'd blown it. He should have moved on by now, but he'd holed up here for the past two weeks instead, indulging in the decadence and sin the Quarter had to offer. He'd gotten cocky, and he'd gotten stupid. He'd been so sure he'd covered his tracks. He was going by a new name, and he always paid in cash.

He'd left Florida five months ago, moving around constantly until he'd landed here. He'd been *safe*, goddamn it! Certain he'd pulled it off. How had they found him?

He shook his head. It still swam from one too many absinthe drips. He pressed a hand to the damp brick to steady himself and swallowed down a flood of acid in his throat. The sounds of revelry and jazz wafted down the alley from Bourbon Street. The air was hot and sweet, saturated with humidity, liquor, and the smells of spicy food.

David sucked in a sharp breath against the bile rising in his throat. Brianna had his files now, the bitch. Panic flooded him. Briefly, he wondered if she would negotiate. If she would consider a cut of the money he'd taken to give them back again.

He put his forehead against the brick and breathed deep. Fuck no, she wouldn't negotiate. He knew that. He'd tried once before when he'd sensed she was as sick of working for Rivera as he was.

But Brianna was tough, and she wasn't caving. And now he was out here with his dick swinging in the wind. He had no guarantees without those files. The money wouldn't do him a damn bit of good if he was dead.

It had taken years to build the dossier. It was his protection, his assurance that Rivera wouldn't send anyone to kill him. So long as he had the files, he was safe. Or so he'd told himself—except that he hadn't quite believed it enough to live out in the open under his own name.

He should have set up an online backup, but he'd been too worried it would somehow fall into the wrong hands. He didn't want evidence of Rivera's crimes—and his by extension—sitting on a server somewhere just waiting for the Feds to find it.

It was different if he traded it for immunity, but to have the Feds get all the info without him having it as a bargaining chip?

Not happening.

Goddamn it!

Right now, he almost wished he'd taken the chance. If he *had* parked those files somewhere online, he wouldn't be standing here and cursing himself six ways to Sunday. He'd only be a simple download away from replacing the evidence, but instead the files were gone and he was as vulnerable as a virgin in a whorehouse.

He should have moved to a new location by now. That was the second dumbass thing he'd done. He'd stayed here when he should have gone south and kept going until he nearly fell off the tip of South America. He was tired of doing Rivera's dirty work, tired of being the brains behind the financials and getting nothing in return. Hell, Rivera hadn't even recognized how valuable an asset he could be.

But David had gotten the last laugh when he'd skimmed a cool ten million for himself out of the Florida operations. He wasn't greedy—Rivera was worth far more—but he wanted his due.

Yeah, he'd run Evie's business into the ground in the process. Maybe he shouldn't have done it. Her paltry earnings were only a drop in the bucket of his ten mil—but it had gotten him what he wanted faster than if he'd waited another few months to skim the money out of Rivera's operations. Simply put, he'd had no choice if he wanted his freedom. And he wanted that far more than he'd wanted anything else.

David shook his head again. It wasn't too late for him yet. Rivera probably thought he had him between a rock and a hard place. But Rivera didn't know a damn thing about him if he believed that.

There were other kinds of backups. Other ways to hide information. David just had to go and sweet-talk Evie one more time. A much more difficult task this time around, not only because she was pissed at him but also because Brianna Sweeney was on his ass.

But desperation had a way of making a man do whatever it took. He *would* get those files back again.

And then he would disappear for good.

THREE

EVIE FROWNED AT herself in the mirror as she turned this way and that.

"You look gorgeous, Evie. Now let's get moving."

Evie turned to her cousin with a sigh. "It's a lovely dress, but I'm not quite sure it's appropriate for an evening at the lake."

What she really wanted was to pull on her faded jeans and a T-shirt, but Julie wouldn't hear of it.

As expected, Julie scoffed. "Please. We'll be at the pavilion—and the other girls will be dressed up too, you'll see."

Julie smoothed a hand over the denim mini she wore. She'd paired it with a silk tank and a pair of pink plat-forms, and she looked gorgeous. Julie was petite and cute, whereas Evie was tall and not so cute.

Evie tugged at the hem of the dress. It was a pale pink color with wide straps and a skirt that was a hair too tight. And short. The three-inch heels Julie had talked her into wearing didn't help either. "It's a bit short, don't you think?"

Julie shook her auburn ringlets. "No. It looks amazing on you! That dress has never looked as good on me. Blush is *so* not my color."

Evie sighed and gathered the tiny purse Julie had insisted she carry. "This really isn't me, Jules. I'm a chef. I work in hot kitchens all day and I wear comfortable clothes."

"You aren't a chef right now," Julie pointed out. "Think of it like you're on vacation. Everybody gets dressed up on vacation, right?"

"Yes, but I don't feel like I'm on vacation."

Julie huffed. "Is this about Matt Girard and what happened back in high school?"

Evie felt a tiny pinch in her chest. "Of course not."

Julie looked militant. "Good. Because that was high school, Evie, and we aren't there anymore. No one gives a good goddamn that you slept with Matt our junior year or that he bragged about it. Half those girls would have dropped their panties in a New York second if they'd thought he'd give them a lay. Still would."

Evie's skin was hot and she wasn't quite sure why. Because Julie was right, and she really didn't give a shit what people thought about her these days—her reaction in the salon notwithstanding. She wasn't sixteen anymore, and she couldn't be hurt by whispers and rumors.

No, her issues with this town were the same issues she'd always had—the ones where she felt like there was a box she was supposed to stay in and she just didn't want to. Aside from that, her only problem today had been coming face-to-face with the boy she used to love and remembering the way he used to make her feel.

"Fine, I'll wear it. Let's go."

"Excellent," Julie replied. "Besides, you look hot— and you want to impress Matt, don't you?"

Evie's stomach bottomed out. "Why would I want to do that?" She waved a hand. "He's old news. Besides, he's not coming, remember?"

Julie laughed, her dark eyes sparkling. "Right. Didn't you see the way he was looking at you today? He'll be there."

"He wasn't looking at me *any* way. We were just talking."

Julie shook her head. "Girl, I think the heat in those kitchens has gone to your head. Matt Girard is just about the hottest thing on two legs, and he was definitely looking at you with interest. He wants in your panties again, trust me." Julie grinned. "And if you're smart, you'll let him."

Evie felt as if her cheeks were six shades of fuchsia. The last time she'd let a man in her panties, she'd lost her damn restaurant. And though the thought of Matt there made her body tingle in ways it hadn't in a very long time, there was no way she was going to repeat the mistakes of her past. They might not be teenagers, and she might not give a damn what anyone said these days since she was no longer vulnerable, but sleeping with Matt was just a bad idea all around.

Her feelings for Matt had always been a giant tangle, like a ball of Christmas lights buried in the garage all year, and she really didn't want to start sorting them out again.

"He won't be there, Jules. Mark my words."

Julie sighed. "Fine. But he will be in town for a few days, so do yourself a favor and don't push him away when he comes around. You definitely need to get laid."

Evie shook her head. "Maybe so, but he's the wrong

man to do it."

Julie snorted. "Well, I can promise you one thing. If he looks at me that way, I'm not saying no."

"Go for it," Evie said, though a little twinge of jealousy speared into her at the thought.

"There's always Jimmy Thibodeaux, if you insist on saying no to Matt. He's been asking after you since he got back."

Evie frowned. Jimmy had been one of the worst back in high school after Matt had left. Always calling her Easy Evie and grabbing her ass. She'd hated him then. She didn't much care for the idea of him now since she'd heard he hadn't changed much. Thankfully, he'd been away in Montana on a hunting trip for most of the month and she hadn't yet had the dubious pleasure of running into him again.

"I'll pass."

Julie shrugged. "Probably best. Jimmy's not been quite right in the head lately. He pulled a knife on Ginny Temple a couple of months ago."

Evie's heart somersaulted. "What do you mean?"

"She said something about his hunting dog crapping on her lawn and Jimmy waved that knife around like he was some kind of avenger. But nothing came of it."

Evie shook her head. Damn crazy Cajun redneck. She hadn't missed that about Rochambeau at all. "And you were seriously suggesting I should sleep with him?"

Julie's mouth turned down. "Of course not! I was kidding. Geez, you've lost your sense of humor lately."

"It hasn't been a good few months, Jules."

"Which is why I said you should get laid. Take your mind right off it. But no Matt and definitely no Jimmy."

She patted Evie's arm. "We'll find someone."

"I'd rather we didn't."

Julie grinned. "We'll see. Now let's stop talking about it and get going."

Evie's little sister looked up from her position in front of the television as they walked through the living room. Evie's heart twisted at the look on the girl's face. Evie had been home a month now, and Sarah was still sullen and withdrawn.

Not that she could blame the kid. There was ten years difference in their ages, and Evie hadn't exactly been around for the past few years. No, she'd been off doing her own thing and calling home on occasion rather than making an effort to be a part of her little sister's life. She hadn't thought of it much at the time, but being home and seeing the effects—well, it made her feel rotten every time she saw that wary look on Sarah's face.

"Where are y'all going looking like that?" Sarah was curious, but her tone said she couldn't care less.

"It's a party." Julie put her hands on her hips. "For adults."

Sarah snorted. "Yeah, I figured that."

"I don't have to go," Evie said, though Julie made a noise when she did. "Is there something you want to do tonight? We could go for pizza, or maybe a movie?"

Sarah turned back to the TV and pressed the channel button. "I ate pizza for lunch. And there's nothing at that lame theater I want to see."

Evie sighed. "Mama's at the Moose Lodge for the evening. Are you sure you don't want me to stay?"

Sarah's eyes flashed. "I know where Mama is. She's been going to bingo every week for the past four years.

Not that *you* would know that."

Julie bristled. "You need to lighten up, little girl. Your sister's had a bad time of it and she could use your support."

Sarah shot to her feet. "Yeah, well why do I have to be nice to her when she's never thought twice about me and Mama? Went off to that fancy cooking school and forgot all about us. Now she's back and thinks we're supposed to care? Like hell." Sarah tossed the remote onto the couch and stalked toward her bedroom.

Julie's dozen or so bracelets clinked as she popped her hands on her hips again and stared after Sarah. "That little brat. You want me to go get her and make her apologize?"

Evie shook her head, even as she swallowed the lump in her throat. "No, forget it. She didn't get mad overnight, and she won't get un-mad that way either."

"Your mama's been too indulgent with her. She would've paddled your behind for acting that way, no matter how old you were."

"Mama's busy, Jules. And I doubt Sarah acts that way toward her. Me, on the other hand…" She sighed. "Maybe if I *had* been here, she wouldn't be so hostile. I can't really blame her for not trusting me."

Julie snorted. "Don't kid yourself, girlfriend. She's a teenager. Brattiness is practically a requirement." Julie tossed her hair over her shoulder and peered up at Evie. "C'mon, you ready to go get laid? That'll certainly help your mood, I promise."

Evie laughed, though inside she still stung from Sarah's rejection. But there wasn't much she could do about it. Even if she stayed here, she'd get nowhere with the kid.

Sarah would hide in her room until Mama came home later. "God no. But I'll go out to the lake with you and have a beer or two. Then I'm coming home. *Alone*."

Julie rolled her eyes. "Your loss. Especially when Matt Girard shows up."

"He's not coming, Julie."

"Bet he does. And when I win, you have to cook your famous gumbo for me."

Evie rolled her eyes. "He won't."

Julie looked smug. "We'll see…"

Rochambeau Lake had a split personality. One side—the side with picnic tables, charcoal grills, and a big pavilion—was clear and calm. But the farther you went across the lake, moss-draped cypress trees crowded together like shadowy sentinels and the lake became a bayou. Gators swam deep in the cypress, down the long winding fingers of murky water that branched and stretched for miles throughout the parish. Snakes coiled in the trees overhanging the water, sometimes dropping in on unsuspecting anglers.

Evie couldn't see the people splashing in the dark, but she heard them laughing. Crazy to go swimming in the middle of the night, even if it was hot. A flash of murky water and the black S-curve silhouette of a snake flowing toward her were the most vivid memories of her last foray into the bayou.

Evie shuddered. She wasn't getting into—or onto—the bayou ever again. She'd never been particularly squeamish, but that afternoon when the snake had fallen out of the tree and into the little canoe—which she and Julie then proceeded to overturn in their panic—had seared itself into her memory.

Just then, Jimmy Thibodeaux reappeared with a beer and a wine cooler, and Evie gritted her teeth. So much for avoiding Jimmy. He'd made a beeline for her the minute they arrived and he hadn't let her out of his sight in the fifteen minutes since. He'd been nothing but polite, however, so she couldn't exactly get away from him without being rude.

And she wasn't prepared to be rude just yet. She kept thinking of him pulling a knife on Ginny Temple, but she didn't think he was crazy enough to do something like that here with so many people around. The other guys would tackle him if he tried it.

Evie craned her neck, looking for Julie, but her cousin had slipped into Steve LaValle's arms and didn't look as if she was slipping out again anytime soon. She didn't think Julie had meant to leave her with Jimmy, but that didn't change the current situation.

"I know you said beer, but I thought you might like this better." Jimmy handed her a wine cooler and sat down on the bench beside her. "I know how you ladies like foo-foo drinks."

Evie's jaw felt like it might crack. "Thanks." She scooted down the bench as much as possible. The crowd closed to hide Julie and Steve from her view.

Damn it.

She turned and tried to smile politely at Jimmy. He

wasn't bad-looking, with his dark hair and dark eyes, but she'd never liked him. He was loud, brazen, and a bit too macho. Always had been. If she had to hear another story about him bagging a gator—or a moose in Montana— she'd probably scream.

"So," Jimmy said, his hand skimming across her bare knee and up her thigh. "You back in town for good?"

Evie pushed his hand away and kept smiling. There wasn't an ounce of friendliness in it, but she knew Jimmy was too dumb to see it. No, he leered and groped like they were back in high school and she was still Easy Evie. More than anything, it made her mad. Livid.

"Nope," she replied through clenched teeth. "I'll be leaving again soon."

She didn't know that for sure, but it was definitely the plan. The sooner, the better. She felt a pang of guilt when she pictured Sarah's sullen face, but that was life. *Her life* dictated that she had to get out of Rochambeau or go crazy.

"That's a shame. Maybe we could get together before you go." He leaned in a little more, his fingers skimming the side of her breast.

Evie shot to her feet, and Jimmy barely managed to catch himself before he fell into her vacant seat. "No, thanks." She said it politely when what she really wanted to do was sock him. "I'm not ready to start a relationship."

"Who said anything about a relationship?" Jimmy blinked up at her, clueless as usual. But there was something in those eyes, something cold and mean. It made her shiver. "You got time for sex, ain't you?"

Warning bells rang in her head as she faced him down. Her smile could have cut glass. Maybe she should have socked him anyway. "Oh darn, I took a vow of celibacy two days ago. Look, there's my cousin."

She spun on her high heels, thankful she didn't trip and make a mockery of her grand exit, and walked away without waiting for an answer. She didn't turn around to look at Jimmy, but she could feel his eyes on her as she stepped into the pavilion. She'd pissed him off, that was for sure.

Evie breathed a sigh of relief as she skirted the makeshift dance floor where couples gyrated to the music someone played using an iPod and two great big speakers. She didn't think Jimmy would pull anything, but she liked having a crowd around her just in case.

She searched for Julie, finally spotting her again. Julie leaned back against Steve, her head on his shoulder, her lips tilted up to accept a lingering kiss.

By the looks of it, Julie wasn't going to be willing to leave just yet. Julie had probably had sex with Steve a thousand times, but they still had to go through this ritual-courting thing first. They got together, broke up, then made up a few days later with wild monkey sex. This looked like a monkey-sex night, but there was a protocol to follow. Why they couldn't just admit they were hot for each other and go for it, Evie would never understand.

Evie set the wine cooler she'd nearly forgotten she was still holding on top of a table as she skirted the crowd. She'd go hang out in Julie and Steve's corner until they were ready to leave. If she were lucky, it'd be a matter of minutes before they couldn't keep their hands off each other and wanted to go back to Steve's place. Before they did, she'd get Julie's keys and drive herself home.

"I think you lost your drink."

Evie knew that voice. It slid over her like hot silk and she spun to find Matt Girard standing behind her, holding the bottle she'd just ditched. Why did her heart skip the second he showed up? And why did he have to look so *delicious*?

"I didn't lose it."

He stood there in faded jeans and a dark T-shirt that molded to his hard pecs and biceps. But it wasn't his clothing that got her attention so much as his eyes. There was something in them, something she didn't remember seeing when he'd been seventeen. He'd been part of this crowd long ago, much more than she had, but he no longer looked like he belonged—in spite of the longing looks some of the women were casting in his direction.

His gaze dropped over her before rising again, slowly, and her body reacted as if he'd brushed his fingers over her. There was something hot, sharp, and thrilling in that gaze—and she was way more susceptible to it than she wanted to be.

Once, she would have given anything for him to look at her like that. Now, she wasn't certain she'd survive the experience.

"Great dress." His voice was silky.

Evie swallowed. She was tingling, and that wasn't a good thing. The last time she'd tingled over this man, it had not turned out so well. "Thanks. I think."

He grinned. "It's definitely a compliment."

Evie crossed her arms and tried to look cool. "Thought you weren't coming tonight."

"Now what made you think a thing like that?"

Her blood slogged like molasses in her veins. "I believe you said 'probably not' in response to Julie's query."

His teeth flashed. "Yeah, but that's before I knew you'd be here."

"What do you want, Matt?" Her heart thrummed like she was sixteen again.

His gaze dropped once more. "Maybe I'd like to see what's under that dress." His voice sounded low and sexy. It pooled in her belly and sent hot waves of need spiraling outward.

"Forget it," she said with a conviction she didn't quite feel. "As I recall, the last time didn't turn out so well for me."

"I know, and I'm sorry."

"You said that earlier."

"I did."

She tossed her hair over her shoulder. "So why'd you come then? I heard you the first time."

He sighed. "Evie. Jesus." He raked a hand through his hair, and her blood hummed at the ripple and flex of muscle. "I just got back from the desert. Life out there is... unpredictable. It makes a man think. And I've decided that I don't like feeling like a shithead for something that happened ten years ago. I want to clear the slate."

Evie let out a breath. She'd been so hurt; then she'd been angry. But it was a long time ago and she couldn't hold a grudge forever. Even now, she recognized that most of her feelings about the incident were still tied up with having her love so cruelly flung back in her face. The other stuff, while definitely unpleasant at the time, hardly mattered anymore.

"We were kids, Matt."

"I hurt you."

She didn't flinch from his gaze. "You did. But I'm

not sixteen anymore. And like I said today, it was my fault too. I asked you to do it. And I told a couple of my friends about it, so it wasn't just you telling the boys." She shrugged with a lightness she didn't quite feel. "What happened was probably inevitable. The guys thought I was easy. The girls who were jealous said I was a slut. They made my senior year difficult in some ways. But what hurt the most was never hearing from you again."

There, she'd said it. She'd told him what really hurt, and she'd given him a window into her feelings back then. He'd have to be an idiot not to know, but it was always possible he hadn't.

"I should have called you."

The music changed, the beat slowing. Evie took a step backward instinctively, but Matt caught her hand and held it tight. She tugged once, then stopped. They faced each other across a few feet of space. Around them, couples began to slide together, fitting into each other.

Evie's pulse beat harder. Her skin sizzled where they touched, his big hand engulfing hers, his palm calloused in a way that shocked her. He was a Girard—rich, entitled— and he had a workman's hands.

"One dance."

Her insides melted a little more. "I'm not sure it's a good idea."

But what she really wanted to do was say yes.

His eyes were bright. "Why not? We're adults now, Evie. No one's getting hurt here."

He said it like it was so easy, but was it really? Wasn't she still vulnerable on some level? She was down on her luck right now, feeling like a loser, and here he was, the same gorgeous, cocky, beautiful creature he'd always been.

Except, no, he was more than that, wasn't he? There was something behind his smile now. Something dark and sad. Pain flared in his gray eyes and then was gone so quickly she wondered if she'd imagined it.

It shocked her. She suddenly wanted to know what had happened to him. She'd heard about him being held captive by terrorists. How could he not be affected by something like that? Of all the things she'd expected Matt Girard to do with his life, putting himself into danger had not even occurred to her. He had everything. Why would he want to risk his life that way?

She remembered when his mother had died. He'd been twelve. Mama had taken her to the wake out at Reynier's Retreat. There were so many people crowding the beautiful rooms of the mansion. The house was heavy with sadness and thick with grief, and it had scared her. She'd escaped to run down the wide lawn. She'd known where to find Matt. He'd been curled inside the hollow of a tree they'd found a few years before.

He'd been dressed in a black suit, his dark hair slicked back carefully, his gray eyes wide and wounded as he looked up at her. Her heart had lifted into her throat then. She'd only been eleven, but she'd felt something in that moment that rocked her world—and would continue to rock her world until she was sixteen and shattered by his casual cruelty.

But not that day. That day, she'd slid into the hollow and sat down beside him. When she'd put her arms around him, he'd turned his face into the crook of her neck and wept.

Evie sucked in a breath. How could she walk away

from him now, knowing there was something behind those eyes? He was hurting again, and she didn't know why.

"One dance, Evangeline," he said softly when she hesitated. "Make a soldier's night. I just got back from the desert a few days ago. I'd like to dance with a pretty woman and forget about that hellhole for a while."

Evie swallowed. "That's not fair."

He grinned. "Because you can't say no now?"

She nodded.

"Good for me then."

"Just one dance and we go our separate ways, got it?" Because she didn't want to feel this tangle of emotions again. This tiny blossoming in her heart that said she was going to be in so much trouble if she didn't shut it down quickly.

"If that's what you want." His voice was rough.

He took her other hand then, ran his palms up her arms to her shoulders. Little sparks of sensation swirled in her belly, lighting her up like the Fourth of July. He pulled her into his arms right there on the edge of the dance floor.

Evie braced her hands against his chest, pressed back when he tried to bring her closer. It was already overwhelming to be so close to him. To feel his heat and hardness next to her body.

To feel everything she'd once wanted so much.

"I don't bite," he murmured. "Unless you want me to."

"Hardly." But heat flowed through her at the thought. Evie closed her eyes. This was insane. Why had she agreed? It was like she'd stepped back in time and gotten caught in all her girlish dreams.

She was in Matt Girard's arms, dancing with him in

public. Poor Evie Baker and the rich senator's son. The boy most likely to succeed and the girl who would never amount to anything. What a pair.

She should have refused, no matter how much she ached for him. No matter how much history flowed between them.

But he'd trotted out that returning soldier line and she'd caved like a fallen soufflé.

She should walk away right now, but she couldn't seem to make herself do so. Instead, she tried to keep distance between them, stood stiffly in his embrace with her hands on his shoulders until he grasped her arms and twined them around his neck. "At least look like you're having fun."

"What if I'm not?"

He laughed. "Pretend."

They swayed to the music without talking. His body was so hard, like he'd been carved from marble. He was lean and lethal, a finely honed military machine. From the hard contours of his shoulders to the flat planes of his abdomen, there wasn't an ounce of softness anywhere on him.

His hands were in the small of her back, caressing her as they moved. She became acutely aware of her breasts pressing against his chest. When she tilted her head back to look up at him, his eyes were intense. She turned away even as a thrill shot through her.

"I've missed you, Evie. I didn't realize how much until I saw you today."

"Don't lie."

"I'm not lying."

A bead of sweat trickled between her breasts and her

skin grew hot. She'd forgotten how steamy Louisiana nights could be. Why did these morons still party at the lake? They weren't teenagers anymore, and they had houses.

"We haven't spoken in ten years. I hardly think you missed me that much."

Matt's hands slid across her back, leaving a trail of flame in their wake. "I said I didn't realize it until today. That's the truth. You were always honest with me, Evie. I liked that. Needed it."

Evie snorted, more to cover the riot of sensations inside her than anything. "You couldn't have liked it that much. You used to sit on me until I cried uncle."

Matt laughed. "Yeah, you really knew how to piss me off back then. But you were my best friend when we were little."

"Until you left private school and started going to Rochambeau Junior High. Then I was persona non grata."

"Hardly. But you were a girl, and I needed to get in good with the guys."

"And the other girls."

He gave her that pretty grin of his. "Yeah, that too."

As if he'd ever had an ounce of trouble in that department. She remembered his first day in public school, how thrilled she'd been to have him there where they could hang out together—and how jealous she'd been when he'd started paying attention to other girls.

"We go back a long ways, don't we?" Her arms around his neck relaxed a little, until it felt almost natural to be dancing with him like this.

"Yeah. It's kinda nice, isn't it?"

Her body was singing and zinging with sparks. "It is,

in a way. In other ways, it's not so great."

He looked puzzled. "How do you mean?"

Evie sighed. "Geez, Matt, you aren't that clueless. It was fun while we were kids. I adored you—and then it changed as I got older and realized what boys were for. But it didn't change for you, and that set me up for a lot of angsty nights discussing you endlessly with my friends."

"You discussed me?" He looked puzzled and she wanted to pinch him. Men.

"Of course. It's what girls do. We like a boy and we obsess about it. About what he said, what he did, how he looked at us. Does he like us or not? Things like that. I wanted you to like me as a girl, not as a buddy. And you never did."

"I did." Her heart did a little skip that it shouldn't have so long after the fact. "But I tried not to. I didn't want to mess up what we had."

"We didn't have anything by then. You'd been ignoring me since I got breasts."

His gaze dropped to her chest and she automatically stuck a finger under his chin and tilted his head up again.

His grin was not in the least apologetic. "Hey, you mentioned them. They are magnificent, by the way."

She refused to feel an ounce of pleasure over that comment. "I did indeed, but that wasn't an invitation to ogle. Focus on my eyes, Girard."

"Such pretty eyes. So blue they're almost purple."

Evie rolled said eyes. "Flattery? After all this time? Care to tell me what's up?"

His expression changed, growing quietly serious. "I wish I could." He gave his head a little shake. "I've seen a lot of bad shit in this world, Evie. You're soft and sweet and you smell good."

There was a lump in her throat. "It's just perfume. You should smell me when I've been picking crabmeat out of shells all day. Or after a long shift on the line, standing over a hot grill—"

"Evangeline."

Evie blinked up at him. "What?"

"You gave me one dance. Do we have to talk about crabmeat and grills?"

Heat slid into her cheeks. "No, I suppose not."

He slid his hands to her hips and pulled her tighter against him until she wanted to whimper. "Good. Because I want to remember this the next time I'm on an op."

Evie dropped her gaze from the heated intensity of his. They moved together silently for a few moments. And then she spoke. "I heard you got shot. Did you really?"

"Yes."

Her eyes flew up again and her heart pounded. "Where?"

"A flesh wound in the side, nothing life threatening. Hurt like hell though."

She shook her head. "I can't understand how you ended up in the military. It's not what I thought you'd do."

His eyes glittered. "And I always knew you'd do something with cooking."

She didn't miss that he'd deflected her comment, but she smiled anyway. "How could you know that? It wasn't like I ever cooked a meal for you when we were swinging from trees or sneaking up on Christina with crawdads."

"No, but you talked about food a lot. About the texture of cupcakes, the correct sweet-to-tart ratio of lemonade, and the heat index of your mama's jambalaya. And then you went to work out at Charlie's that summer before my senior year. I brought Jeanine Jackson on a date there, remember?"

Evie had to stifle a groan. "God, how could I forget? I dumped a pitcher of sweet tea down her shirt. But that had nothing to do with cooking."

Matt laughed. "No, it sure didn't. What did she say to you again?"

"I think *you bitch* is about right. Or some variation of that phrase."

"No, I mean before that. Before you 'tripped' and lost control of the tea."

Evie sighed. "She gave me a dirty look and told me not to talk to her boyfriend if I wasn't taking his order."

"Was that it?" His brows drew down as if he were thinking back. "I thought for sure it must have been something worse."

"I didn't like her tone."

Matt snickered. "Sounds about right. You never did back down from a fight."

The song ended then and Evie took a step backward. Matt's grip on her tightened, but then he let her go, his hands dropping to his sides. Evie swallowed. "Thanks for the dance. It was nice."

His gaze was so intense she wanted to look away, but she didn't. "It doesn't have to end here. I'm home for a few days. I want to see you again, Evie."

Her heart ricocheted around her chest. "I don't think it's a good idea."

He shook his head. "You keep saying that to me, *chère*, but your eyes say something different."

She clasped her hands together and took a deep

breath. "I've always been weak where you're concerned. But too much time has passed and there's too much drama when you're involved. I've got enough going on in my life without adding you to the mix."

His expression sharpened. "Are you seeing someone?"

She wished she could say yes, wished it were true just long enough to make him go away. And she didn't, because she didn't want him to go away.

Geez, way to be strong, Evie.

"It doesn't matter. Besides, you're leaving in a few days. What would be the point in spending any time together?"

"I think you know the point." His voice was a deep, sexy growl, and she felt an answering throb in her belly and her sex.

Impulsively, she stepped forward and squeezed his hand while she gave him a peck on the cheek. He turned his head and their lips met, but the contact was too brief as she backed away again, her heart hammering in her throat and ears.

"Goodbye, Matt."

Evie turned to go just as the lights in the pavilion snapped out. She stumbled to a halt as the crowd gasped. Scattered headlights illuminated the area, but not enough to see more than a few inches.

A car backfired, and Evie nearly leapt out of her skin. Someone screamed, and then a chorus of screams erupted when the car backfired again. The crowd surged, knocking her off balance. A hand wrapped around her arm and tugged her up against a hard chest.

"We have to get out of here." It was Matt's voice in

her ear and she turned her head, prepared to ask him why—until the car backfired again and she realized what was really happening.

That wasn't a car. It was a gun.

ABOUT THE AUTHOR

Lynn Raye Harris is the *New York Times* and *USA Today* bestselling author of the HOSTILE OPERATIONS TEAM SERIES of military romances as well as 20 books for Harlequin Presents. A former finalist for the Romance Writers of America's Golden Heart Award and the National Readers Choice Award, Lynn lives in Alabama with her handsome former-military husband, two crazy cats, and one spoiled American Saddlebred horse. Lynn's books have been called "exceptional and emotional," "intense," and "sizzling." Lynn's books have sold over 3 million copies worldwide.

Connect with me online:

Facebook: www.facebook.com/AuthorLynnRayeHarris
Twitter: https://twitter.com/LynnRayeHarris
Website: http://www.LynnRayeHarris.com
Email: lynn@lynnrayeharris.com

Join my Hostile Operations Team Readers and Fans Group on Facebook:
https://www.facebook.com/groups/HOTReadersAndFans/

LynnRayeHarris.com

Made in the USA
Middletown, DE
06 December 2018